Dare You?

A gothic anthology by gifted young writers.

*RPA Young Publishers is an independent student-run
organisation operating within Richmond Park Academy.*

Editor in Chief: Charlotte Cubitt
Collection subeditors: Sophie Heath, Tippi Wilson, Kyrill Potapov, Kiya Weekes
Artistic editor: Sophy Higgins
Marketing and sales: Tainton Cole, Ethan Connolly

Cover art: Charli Eglinton

ISBN 978 0 9576981 0 9 (Paperback)
978 0 9576981 1 6 (eBook)

Foreword

The work in this collection forms a fine and intricate web, capturing many of the subtle images, uncanny narratives and pure spirit associated with the genre of Gothic Fiction. The authors (all twelve or thirteen at time of writing) have delved deep, traversing the tradition from Browning to Freud, from the re-imagining of Classical Myth to the mystery of the Orient, from the 16th Century to the present day.

When I first read the manuscript given to me by RPA Young Publishers (the student executive team behind this project), I was struck by the vitality of its voices. Rather than editing out every grammatical quirk, maximizing clarity or smoothing over rough edges, I have endeavoured to preserve the authenticity of every voice. How is it that our young writers can invent such complex and empathic fiction? Perhaps being thirteen is not so different from being the hero of a Gothic Romance in a changing and boundless world.

These stories are not for the faint-hearted. Dare you enter these pages? Dare you become a guest of these worlds?

-Kyrill Potapov, Project Coordinator

Contents

The Night Dance
Mary Beaty

The wind whistled
Floating through the air
Leaves swirling
Captured by the breeze.

A shining moon
Gives no light
To the endless
Seeking blackness.
Trees sway
To the tune of the blackness
Birds screech
And take off in flight.
The lake
All still in the darkness
Silently waits
For the waves of sunlight.

The leaves dance
In the hollow night
The endlessness
Is blinding.

A thin path,
Muddy with footprints
Waiting to be flattened
By the few people passing.

A hedge of brambles
Sorrowful and weary
It's only rest
Is the little, night dance.

A single cloud
Hugging the moon
Alone and waiting
For the sun to rise.
A star
Attempting to shimmer
Through the thickening
Black sky.
The grass on the ground
Growing its strength
Ready to be trampled
To a bruised and beaten
heap.

An old thatched cottage
Hammered and worn
It waits for the day
To get pounded even more.
The movement of the night
The dancing and songs
All gone by the day
When they're dreary and
frayed.

--

The Cruel Heart
Sophie Heath

Once upon a time, there lived a handsome, charismatic and charming young Earl. This young man owned an enormous and beautiful span of land, and was hugely rich. He planned to marry and share his fortune with his beloved sweetheart, but unexpectedly, just before their marriage, she died – leaving him lonely and full of hate.

From that day onwards, he decided that he could never love again, for fear of the excruciating and overpowering feeling of hurt returning. And so, to guarantee his wishes were met, he ripped out his heart, encasing it in a grand chest at the centre of his opulent estate.

Years later, and the rich man had grown cold and cruel, intent only on making more money to add to his colossal fortune. Now close to death, he found himself needing a wife. He needed an heir to his wealth as he had no kin to pass it on to. Who could bear the thought of it all being seized by the fat mayor and his people?

Confident in his good looks and money, but desperate in his old age, he walked into the village, determined to return to the castle with a fiancé. Spotting a pretty looking girl on the bridge, he swaggered towards her in a disinterested manner. The question was out: would she marry him?- and the answer: no;

no? How on earth could she have possibly said no? He was attractive and rich, what more could she ever have hoped for?

"How could I love such a cruel man, you believe your looks can get you everywhere? You're wrong. You believe your money can get you everywhere? You're wrong. I am already in love, besides." Walking towards her small cottage, she slammed the door behind her.

The man stood there, not shocked but pleased, the girl had planted a seed of thought in his head that bubbled and boiled like the final ingredient in a soup. Grotesque visions came forth – thoughts soaked in blood and cunning.

And with these thoughts, circulated a plan.

In the night, whilst the girl slept, he would cut the throat of the only man she cared for and the only person who gave her shelter, leaving her no choice but to seek refuge with him.

The plan took place just as it was formed; no-one suspected anything, none questioned his innocence. The silent night was broken only by the rasping of a crow and the whispering wind.

The following morn, as the Earl swaggered over the crumbling frost, he congratulated himself on his genius. He walked back to the rickety bridge. He spotted the pretty pauper crying, and paused, seeming confused. Why should she be crying after all? She had a life of wealth mapped out for her, what had she to be sorry for? "Come with me," he said steadily, "be my wife, there's nothing left for you here."

The girl rose, shocked and bewildered. "How could I love a man who has no heart? How could I give my love to someone who would only return cruelty, for you can give me no love."

"Come," The man said coldly, "and I will give my heart in return for your own," he added calmly, "that's a promise."

And so they walked towards the looming castle, a man and a girl.

Arriving at the castle, the man busied himself opening an enormous oak chest.

Eventually, the great doors creaked open and he showed the girl a blood red pumping heart, wired into what seemed to be a large machine.

The girl opened her mouth to scream, but before a sound was heard, the man leapt forward, and slitting her chest open, lifted her dripping sparrow of a heart out in a victorious gesture. The girl sank to the floor. The man cut his own chest and replaced her heart in the empty hollow on the left of his torso, and cried, "At last! An heir to my estate!"

A Feather
Chimera Van Rhyn

All I could see in the dimness of my room was the fragile little silhouette on the floor and the swirls in the black shadows too deep for my eyes to understand. I scoop the tiny bundle with both hands, and although I notice the downy feather that floats away on a breeze, I cannot feel, I do not reach for it. Every time I return here, this breeze carries memories. On other nights I would have raced to light the candles as if their wavering light was my only saviour, but tonight I savour the darkness and hold tightly the frigid body of the young bird. A few minutes ago it was the prey of the Black Cat. Despite this feline appearing larger at every encounter, I had no idea where he was being housed and fed.

Although I felt the urge to begin my search outside, I had not considered what this journey entailed or what drove me to this fever of determination. Nevertheless, I followed my first thought and arrived in the garden. Even when moonlit, the contrast between the top and ground floors of the mansion was striking - it was as though two separate quarrelling architects had stacked their works one on the other. Many times I had stood in the garden and studied the differences, but tonight I felt like I was the subject being studied. I traced my gaze up along the ivy; the brickwork turned a darker brown and the windows became arched and beautifully ornate. My eyes tracked down the culprit infuriatingly out of my reach in the attic window. A familiar thought made its way into my mind: he had no right to invade my home, and further break our once found trust! Unlike most, I use to believed black cats were a sign of luck, not a bad omen.

Still he stood emotionless, peering out at me in this windy night. I cautiously edged towards the house when without warning, as if with a howl, the back door slammed shut, making him spring back to life. For a second he turned away with his owl-eyes still watching me, then leaped as if about to take off in flight. He swooped silently back into the house, claiming it for himself. Previously I simply assumed that the Black Cat lived far away from here. But tonight had proven that we lived closer than I could ever anticipate. By the time I found myself at the front door I knew that I would not find calm if I did not make it my mission to know where the Black Cat resided.

Despite this revelation I still could not enter my own home. Sure enough I spotted an invitingly open window, on the second floor. Inconveniently, my ladder was around the back but I had no other straightforward choices unless I retrieved it. Upon collecting the ladder, I discovered that the back door was not, as I had assumed, locked. Sighing because of the wasted time, I entered. I was relieved to be back at home, though the pest had still not been dealt with. Since the invader had revealed its location, I didn't think it would be difficult to find him. BlackCat, however, decided to lead me through the maze of rooms himself.

I took the stairs to the next level, observing the carpet that would have looked brand new if it didn't lie beneath a layer of dust. Together with the raised temperature on the second floor, the dust layer seemed to suffocate everything, including myself. As I continued along the landing, I passed the ornate doors that line the corridors and crowd this otherwise empty space. When had I last been up here, and why did none of it bring back memories? I climbed the next staircase and spotted the first trace of Black Cat: a cluster of tiny paw shapes imprinted in the dust leading to a single bold black door against the pale walls. The paws were so small, but I recognised Black Cat's extra toe. The door emitted a sense of menace as I approached it. My shirt snagged on the stair railing, a warning, but then from behind the door I heard a mewing. Against all logic I still stepped forward, grasped the door handle and twisted it.

On entering the room the temperature dropped and with it came the breeze, memories flooding in. The clockwork bear, the rocking horse, the birdcage. I could hear the night clearly - the hush of wind rustling the great oak's leaves accompanied the melody of a desolate nightingale. Twisting and intertwining between the objects I saw a curve of tail - here, there. Multiple paws pad around the room, now seeping together, forming more solid patches of darkness. I take what feels like my last chance to cross the room, shadows consuming every corner, and kneel down by the smooth metal birdcage. A downy feather rests on the knotted wood floorboards, forcing my eyes up to the cage, its door swinging free.

The black cat separates itself from the dark, padding calmly out of the door. All I could see in the dimness of my room was the fragile little silhouette on the floor and the swirls in the black shadows, too deep for my eyes to understand.

Awakening
i. Ellie Still

I never believed in magic until the day I saw a book shimmering gold and green from the shelf; it caught my eyes and dragged me towards it. As I reached up and pulled the book out from the shelf, I read: Desire of Magic. It was love at first site, I rushed over to the counter before anyone else could take it, and it was mine. I placed the shiny coins in the frail old ladies wrinkled hands as she gave me a nod of agreement as I danced away, nervous at what could happen. I sprinted home as fast as the wind could take me, as fast as my feet could carry me.

I put the key in my front door, slowly unlocking the future, my heart beat faster by the second. I was desperate to be alone with my book. The door finally opened and I heard a familiar voice behind me; it was Mrs Weekes the young receptionist from a few doors down, she could talk for ages, I didn't have the time for her right now. I was a polite girl as always, I said hello, I think she gathered the idea I didn't want to talk and she said she'd leave me to my duties. Finally, I stepped into my house and slammed the door behind me, now was my chance to run upstairs and have time alone with my book, with only my teddies staring down!

As I opened the book it was like it was part of me already; page after page, word after word, the spells were unfolding. I started learning the spells. Day after day, night after night I studied. I began to forget what was going on around me. There may have been knocking on the door or phone calls but I only thought any of this when one morning I found myself awoken from a dream. I went down stairs as I heard a loud dropping noise. I found it was only my kitten Smokey lying on the kitchen floor. I went to see if she was ok. She purred. I smelt burning from upstairs. My room. Running up the stairs as fast I could, I pushed opened my door to notice that only the window was covered by the flames. Slowly, the rain fell upon the transparent window, clearing the fire into words quoting a spell that I had often studied, "Bide in Loki law ye must, in perfect love and perfect trust, eight words the Loki Reed fulfil: An ye, harm none, do what ye will. What ye sends forth come back to thee, so ever mind the law of three, follow this with mind and heart, Merry ye' meet and Merry ye part."

As I finished reading the spell, the flames covered me without pain and carried me. I knew I wouldn't be returning to my room.

---

ii. FJ

I was walking through the forest. The moon's loneliness
appealed to me. My feet making a crunching noise through the
leaves, old dark souls filling the cold air around me. It was
there... I saw it. There it was, the CHEST. The key to my
destiny and fortune was just a few yards away from me. I opened
the chest with a click and there it was. The book. With this I
could bring my brother back to life and we could reign terror
over the world.

I tried the spells for an hour, and none of them seemed to
work. I flicked angrily to the last page and I saw a name. "This
must have been the author" I said to myself. "I have to go find
him." It took me forty nights and forty days to find this
mysterious magician man. I paddled in my creaking wooden
boat, asking at every harbor. I Eventually found him out on the
rocks off the coast of a small town, by an old misty tower that
may have once been a lighthouse. It was as if he could sense my
presence.

"Sir I need your help in the dark arts, I have this book" I
shouted, trying to be heard over the roar of the crashing waves.

"Why?" snapped the magician.

"For my family" I replied.

"Ok then, let's begin."

I was trained in the dark arts for three years, while, as every second passed, my brother was rotting in his grave. Now it was time to raise my brother from the dead and return to my home town. I searched at the graveyard close to where I and my family lived when I was a kid to try and find my brother's gravestone. I was holding a slowly dying rose to put by my brother's grave in his honour, as I had done for many years before. There I saw it, the gravestone. The dates had faded. He was only 30. I placed the rose down by the grave and took out the spell book. As I started reading the spell my blood turned ice cold and I felt like I could faint but I still carried on reading: "Immortal we will stand, together we will rule this land, side by side, hand in hand, together we will rule this land."

The moon light shone upon my brothers gravestone as fog started to rise around me. I couldn't see anything except the grave. Suddenly the ground started to shake like a raging horse. Suddenly my brother's hand grew through the soil and here was his wedding ring, but something was wrong. Where was his tanned skin? His flesh? The skeleton started to rise out of the ground. As it did so, I toppled to the ground. It made me sick that this could be my twin.

The body was floating in the air, completely lifeless. Then it fell to the ground motionless. I walked to it. The heart wasn't pumping and although a lot of the body was still covered by skin, it was pale white. He looked even more dead than when I killed him. Only his smile remained.

---

iii. Jayden Bruce

I awoke to a light tapping and the sensation that a draft that had
filled the whole room. Branches were banging against my
windows and I concluded that this action must have forced one
open, enough for the slight breeze I still felt on my face. I
opened my eyes and sat up. My windows were masked with
condensation. I knew I had overslept when I saw the big hand
hit 11; 00. I wondered why the heaters were not on yet, but
decided to stop wondering and put on a pair of socks. As I
walked over to my dresser I saw a brown book sitting on top of
my book case, just pointing out. I thought maybe my dad had
got me a new book to read but this was different; it didn't look
new; it was brown and had gold lines and writing on it; but it
looked slightly familiar; but that didn't look like any foreign
language I knew. So I picked it up and headed downstairs. My
dad was gone. Then I remembered he must have taken Peter to
the dentist.

As I flicked through the pages, I felt like I knew what the
weird letters said. It sounded like a book of recipes or poems, or
spells. As I started to say the words that I saw on the page my

body felt different, like what I was doing was giving me a purpose. The words that I was saying were starting to glow a bright blue. As I got halfway through the spell dad bust in and demanded to know where I got the book. I had heard the door open downstairs but I had not taken notice because I was too into the book. I told him it was on my book case and I was sure that someone gave it to me as a gift. He gave a long sigh and sat me down and explained to me what the book does and has in it and why I he didn't want me to know about it. The book was ancient and belonged to my ancestors who passed it down from generation to generation but he said he didn't want me to have it, that there were too many bad people in the world who wanted to be bigger and stronger and if it got into the wrong hands it wouldn't be good for mankind. He claimed it was more of a curse than a gift. I realised my grandparents had taught the language of the book in the lullabies they sang to me, they knew I may need it someday. He told me that when he was my age he used to read the book all the time and sometimes help close some crimes that the police never bothered to handle. I don't know why he let me keep it.

I took good care of it all day like dad asked. Coming back from school, I was about to open the gate when I noticed the front door was wide open and looked like it had been broken - with more force than any good old kick could muster. It had a big black burn around the frame. The furniture was shattered. Dad's watercolour paintings had shrivelled into dust balls.

"Dad?" I shouted "Where are you?" I looked upstairs and heard breathing coming from the bathroom but I couldn't see them. Then I saw dad,

"The book" he demanded, "The book, where is the book?"

It's was in my bag, that was still flung over my shoulder. I grabbed the book out of my bag and slammed my door.

"What have you done with my book?" Dad said through the door.

"It's your book. I never wanted it so why did you bring it to me?"

"I never gave it to you. Now open this door and give me the book!"

"Then will you calm down? I want to know what happened. Let's sort this out before my brother gets home."

I opened the door.

"There, take your book. It's over." I said.

"No it's not, it's only just begun." said a deep voice from the book as it glowed red.

I threw the book at the wall behind dad. The weird language from the book started to leak out and creep up dad's leg. Dad became covered in its words. The book was now gone, My eyes scrambled around the hall to look for it. I realised it was inside him. I screamed out but no one heard me, Again, he started mumbling that weird language. What to do, what to do?

I charged at him but he only fell over. Fortunately it was for long enough for me to get to the door. As I leapt through the hole, dad stood behind me. His eyes glowed blue, then red, just like the words in the book. He was saying them over and over. A blue hole appeared on the hallway ceiling. It sucked in a pillow, then a whole chair. Dad tried to hold on to a table leg but he started to fade away sink into the hole. I had to run. Had to leave. Had to find somewhere where I could live alone and spend my days trying to understand.

"I love you dad." I mouthed.

Thus his body disappeared into the vortex. Pooof! He was gone. And again that mysterious book just sat there.

---

iv. Sophy Higgins

The tragic day my mother died was the worst day of my life. My ignorant father left us when we were little. He walked right out and left our mother to look after us on her own. When we were eight, our mother passed away in a deadly house fire, making my sister Jasmine and me, Amalie, orphans. Five years later, I'm still in this hell people call an orphanage. I'm lonely, bored and missing Jasmine.

Last year, I had an idea which I shared with Jas. I had been searching through the abandoned library and saw a book. I took Jasmine to the bedraggled library where I had found it. It was right where I left it, the green polished leather sparkling in the sunlight. Squinting, Jas managed to work the inscription 'Desire of Magic'. Jas looked up at me staring,

"What's this meant to be Ams?"

"Well don't you miss mum Jas, don't you wish she was here? I do! Every night I cry myself to sleep! I want our mum back Jas and I'm going to get her whether you help me or not." I blurted out. I knew what Jas was going to say. She was going to say I was out of my mind, I was stupid. Jasmine never liked my ideas. We were twins and Jas was 10 minutes older. She was the one with all the smart ideas and the sensible plans.

"I'm sorry; I didn't know you felt like that. I wish you didn't. So how are we meant to get her back?" she mumbled. She was going to agree! My idea was actually going to happen.

"Just meet me at the cemetery at 12 o' clock tonight with the book, I'll take care of the rest" I said, excitedly. Jas looked at me reluctantly and walked out the room. "I'll meet you tonight, but if this is a bad idea and we get in trouble, I'm blaming you Ams."

I waited in the darkness of the cemetery. It got later and later and I grew more and more afraid. Finally at 12:45 Jas turned up.

"I wasn't going to come but I knew you were here and you missed mum, so I turned up and I did what you said. I bought the book, for you."

I glared at her.

"Well come on then, mum's not going to get here on her own."

I threw her a shovel and she started digging. CLINK. She hit the coffin and we saw the shining plaque.

It read: "In loving memory of Crystal Swan, a brilliant mother and amazing friend". Tears rolled down my cheek and I thought about the loneliness I had suffered without my mother. Jasmine didn't look very pleased. "What now?" Jas said calmly. Now we bring back the person who's been dead for five years who you never even talk about. That's what I thought, that's what I wanted to say! "Now we bust it open and say the spell. What else would we do?" I yelled. "Do you even miss her?"

She nodded. "Do you want help? Be quiet or you can go through with this god-awful naive idea on your own. It isn't like it will work anyway." She bellowed angrily in reply. I flipped the lid of the coffin. Jas and I both coughed and spluttered. We both held our noses at the foul stench that was released. I couldn't bear to look at mum like that, with her skin hanging off her face. Flies hovered all around her and perched on her cheek.

We read quickly and watching as she began to stir.

"Given life and given hope, awaken to the world, Vivificasti et datum sperare, evigilare faciatis ad mundum" we repeated over and over. Under the glinting moonlight, a sudden poof of smoke surrounded the area of my mother's grave. A slim figure arose from the soil and stood under the shining moon. It was our mother! Our plan had worked and our mother was back. "Mum!" Jas and I cried, happily. Mum spun round and looked at Jasmine and she opened her gaping mouth like she wanted to bite us. "Children" she grinned. "How nice of you to do this for me. Why don't we go for some dinner? I know the best place." she smiled. I did it. Jas and I did it. We had our mum back and I couldn't be happier. The three of us walked, Jas and me following our joyful mother.

We ended up in the middle of a deserted forest. "Where are we?" Jas asked suspiciously. I wondered why Jas asked mum in such a suspecting manner. "Well children... We're here for dinner of course!" she replied. What did she mean? There was nothing here! Jas grabbed me and pulled me backwards. As mum approached me, a look of complete evil filled her face. She was like a complete stranger. A murdering stranger.

"What are you doing? We brought you back to life so Ams and I could enjoy our lives again. Not so you could... so you could eat us! Is that what's going on here! How could you!" Jas exclaimed in disgust.

"I didn't tell you to bring me back to life, did I? It's your own fault. Did you think you'd dig up love? I never loved you anyway you stupid children. I couldn't be mean to you in case you told someone. But here's something you didn't know Amalie. Jas knew I hated you. I was mean to her because I could be! She was older than you and I knew she wouldn't say anything as she knew how much you hated me!" she growled. I burst into tears. I looked at Jas in disbelief and Jas tried to smile at me sympathetically.

"Now come here girls or I'll do something you'll regret." she laughed.

"RUN!" Jas shouted. That's what we did but it wasn't good enough. I was never fast and mum was 10 times speedier than me. I turned to see mum behind me. She grabbed my neck and I felt her cold killer hands clench into me.

"I told you this would happen." she chuckled. Her mouth swiftly moved towards my neck as if she was going to bite me. "ARGHH!" mum screamed in pain. I was released from her devil hands and she fell to the ground. I saw Jas behind her covered in mud and dirt.

"You can hurt me but you are never going to hurt Amalie! You don't know how much she missed you and you go and do this. You're just a spiteful waste of foul breath. I'm glad you're dead!" Jas screamed. Jas turned and hugged me. I was glad because I sure as hell needed it. But soon after I regretted it.

Jas let go of me and fell to the ground. She was dead. My sister was dead! "What have you done?" I screamed in anger. "I hate you!" I couldn't believe it! She was so young! I grabbed a sharp piece of rock and stabbed my evil mother in the heart. She was dead! I ran home to the orphanage where I saw the hall supervisor. "What's wrong?" she said in a soothing manner. "Jasmine's... Jas is dead" I cried. "Don't worry sshhh, I'm sure she's not really dead"...

Now eight months later, I'm still here. No mum. No Jas. What was I supposed to do! I had no one! When I heard the knock, I answered. "Come in" I sighed. A strange man with slick, brown hair, shuffled in. "Who are you?" I wondered.

"I'm your dad Ams. I'm so sorry I haven't seen you for all this time! Your mum threatened to kill you both if I didn't leave. I tried to call the police, but your mother lied and told them that I had schizophrenia!" he replied. I couldn't believe it! My dad! Finally I had someone.

"Did they tell you what happened?" I asked.

"Yes. But don't worry, I've spoken to them and you can come and live with me. Everything will be fine" he smiled. I had a second chance. At least that's what I hoped.

---

v. Kyron Marcano

I never believed in destruction until I laid eyes on this book. I found it the day I was made an orphan - when my brother and my dad disappeared.

It was the last day of the school term and I didn't realise what surprises lay ahead. As soon as the teacher said we could go, I ran outside, unlocked my bike and rode all the orphanage. I needed to get to my room quickly. The weird thing about the orphanage was that the area it covered becomes dark before sunset. When it rained, the rain hit the orphanage before it hit the rest of the town. All the other kids would stay away. I had no friends, the other children in the orphanage were so young or so strange. I might as well have gone to live in the lighthouse.

I ran up to my room to see the book on my bed a royal blue colour with red detail all over. I opened it to the first page. It said that if I want to live forever I had to cast a certain spell. My life was already miserable enough without living forever. Another spell offered wealth. But I knew not to trust anyone who offered me wealth. For some reason I took the temptation and carried on reading the book. It was just one sentence that struck me. No more than eight words. I had found a spell for love and guessed that perhaps this was what I wanted. So I said the spell - although the language was old fashioned, and went to bed without much more thought. When I woke up I decided to give the book to the library. It only reminded me of the evil and mystery of my past. Perhaps someone else would find hope in it, I thought. The librarian took it without questions and I thought I would never see the book again.

The next day, I met Alice. There was just something about her. We told each-other secrets. She had duties as a cleaner, she still played with her dolls. Two years later we were married. We had two beautiful twins. Then one evening I caught her reading a book she had stolen from the library many many years ago.

I told her she didn't need it and I took it from her. I read it again and considered that living forever and being rich might not be such a bad thing. I read all the spells my own way. I didn't see the spells my wife was talking about. I went to sleep that night thinking how funny it was how the book was back in my life and how it had got into my head.

I woke up the next morning warm, the sunlight shining through the massive windows I own. I walked over to what seemed to be my wardrobe excited realising my floor was made of marble. I got dressed in the best clothes I could find in it. When I ran outside, I saw that my house was the only house alight before dawn. Now at last I was better than the people who had mocked and shunned me. There was a beggar on the street.

I pushed her over and kicked her. She probably would have died even if I didn't help.

I carried on smiling. This smile was eternal. Here were two of the bullies from my secondary school just coming out of their rubbish little home. I had a handy revolver in my pocket. Then three other people and I ran back into my house. I laughed so loud someone came out around the corner. She looked at me with love in her eyes.

I said to her "Who are you?"

"Your love." She said.

"My love is here" I said, and handed her the book. She asked me to leave and I left her. I went in search for a bigger house or a starving man to show off my suit to. Then I too felt hunger and as I lie dying I wonder why my suit is filling with blood. Perhaps the spell did not work as I planned because Alice had cut out those two words for me.

---

vi. Denis Efovi

It was a cold night. I was lying on my bed, thinking about my family. Something was making me think, something bad, something I shouldn't probably know anything about.

It all started yesterday when I found this old book, it had some words in it but the letter were new to me. The only thing I could read was "Perosak" but who knew what it meant. I hid the book under my bed and went to sleep and now here I am, at 2.00 in the morning, still awake. The branches are scraping against the windows making a screeching sound, there are shadows all over my room, they look like monsters in the dark. My room is a complete disaster, clothes all over the floor, my computer still turned on and my dirty socks all over the place.

There was a light noise on coming from downstairs, I tried not to feel too worried about it because it might have been just a bottle or maybe a mouse moving. Then it grew louder. It wasn't noise, it was a mixture of different voices speaking in a foreign language, they sounded scared.

When I was down there, in the kitchen, the old book was on the floor, its pages were glowing red and letters were pouring in and out. The floor and walls were covered in flying letters. They red ink dripped and splashed into new letters. Each letter made a terrifying sound when it hit the book, a scream or a moan.

I took a step forward, then another one, then another one, until I was one step away from it. I could hear all the voices and all of their stories. I had to put my hands on my head to avoid getting mad.

I decided to close the book, which was the wrong thing to do because when I closed it, the walls of the house started burning. The burning letters wrapped around me but it didn't hurt. I was carried somewhere. To my childhood park. I thought I could wash them off in the little pool but it was already filled with people. There were dozens of people all covered in these strange letters, their eyes were white, there was no life in them, the letters were part of their skin and they were glowing bright blue. Then something popped up in my mind, I had a feeling that someone could explain this to me, someone I knew.

After running for about half an hour I found his house I knocked but nobody answered so I just kicked the door with a trembling leg. Inside I found Dr Wilson, an expert of medicine, I knew I could ask him anything and he would probably know the answer, he looked at me as if I was going to kill him, then his eyes brightened and he said:

"Oh my dear, you're not one of them! You are one of us!"

I was confused, I mean, I knew that the city was infected but what did he mean by "us"? I asked him to explain what was happening here, and after listening to his story, I was so worried and so angry that I couldn't even show it. Basically, we had been invaded by these creatures, the "Perosak" They fed on hate, greed and fear. Ideas were forming in my head, I was angry, I was scared, I was worried.

Then something hit me from behind, something cold,

something full of evil.

When I woke up, I was in a cage, hanging over a pit of lava, Dr Wilson was next to me, he looked beaten up. Blood was flowing from my back, but that wasn't the bad thing, oh no, there were hundreds of infected people watching us, then the King, I suppose, played three chords on an organ and Dr Wilson was grabbed by four guards and brought right in front of the crowd, everyone was laughing and cheering. The King had the book in his hand, he read out something and Dr Wilson started transforming, his eyes flew into the pit and were replaced by the giant red eyes of an animal. His body bent and grew. The real Dr Wilson had melted and new, evil marks covered in golden blood flew out of him. Dr Wilson had been used as a sacrifice to make the Perosak stronger, he was the only source of information I had and now he was gone. If only I had read the book differently. I closed my eyes and remembered all the happy things that happened in my life, all ruined by them, my life was a disaster, I was frustrated, so I just let myself fall into the Perosak's bloody, evil hands.

---

vii. George Alden

I had spent weeks planning my holiday, but now I was starting to regret it. It was a cold, stormy morning in the Nokuma village, colder than usual. I dragged myself out of bed, put on my slippers and struggled down the stairs. As I went to put on my kettle something told me not to, I just had a feeling. So instead of that I opened up my curtains. I looked out with astonishment as I could only see white: white trees, white cars, a white house, even the lighthouse out on the little island was white. Snow covered everything visible. There must have been a bad snow storm last night. It was just my luck. On the day I was meant to be going home I get trapped inside this little cabin.

I heard a noise but stayed by the window, watching a car skid and struggle through the snow away from this village. The noise grew louder and louder. I tried to think nothing of it but as it grew louder and louder, I grew apprehensive. I realise that it was someone banging against my door with their both palms. I really didn't want to open it but I knew I had to, this person was sobbing. As I took a deep breath I pushed myself forward, opened the latch and threw open the door. There was no one there. There was the noise again, it had to be my door, the closest house was a mile away. I looked out again. There was no one there, but when I looked down, the corner of a book peered through the snow. It was quite a big book, about the width of a dictionary. I picked it up assuming that someone had misplaced it, but I was wrong. It had my name in big red letters across the back. I dropped the book in shock, what did this mean?

I frantically walked backwards and forwards, trying to think why my name would be on a book. I had never written a book. I had never been a fan of writing or reading. I forced myself to open it. As soon as I did I saw picture of this dog-like animal, it looked like a mythical creature: it had a silvery, black body with bright white teeth and red eyes; not small red eyes BIG red eyes. I knew I couldn't stay here so I rushed back upstairs, packed a light bag of clothes and headed outside the door. I would walk somewhere. The cold air smashed against my face, I could hardly see two feet in front. I don't know how I was meant to get out of this village. With every step came a moment of fear, my heart pounced like a wolf after its prey. Not knowing if I was about to get run over by a car or attacked by that THING, I hated the sound of the squelching noise as my boot stepped in the snow; it sent a tingling feeling up my spine. I had no sense of the time, where I was or even where I was going, I was completely lost.

It was finally night time, but fortunately this place never went completely dark thanks to the lighthouse, although this still wasn't a lot of help in this crazy pounding snow. I was not safe to go further. I found a place to rest tonight, it was inside the hollowed bark of an ancient oak tree. I didn't know if it was home to a bear or a jaguar or even that THING but perhaps I was not being rational. I had to take my chances and spend the night. I had a rough idea of when I woke up. The birds were chattering in the trees like they did every morning. I packed up my sleeping bag and set of for the day. I had to get home, I had to. Luckily, the snow had calmed down a bit so it was easier to see. In the distance I could see a light way above the ground. It must have been the lighthouse and I could have used it to guide me. As I slowly got closer to the light I heard the sound of a plane, the vibration made my knees go weak and I fell to the ground. This plane must have been very big or very low to the ground. I got back to my feet straight away and carried on to the air field, when I got there it was completely abandoned. There were destroyed planes everywhere. It must have been a testing site. Maybe they tested had durable the planes could be in case there was a war or something. I edged closer to one of the destroyed planes but there was a loud sound like a wrench had dropped. It came from the garage, so without thinking I walked towards it. What if there was a person who could help? What if he was cutting up his victims and eating them, but I just forgot that and carried on. I saw a shadow, the person was big, VERY big.

I backed away as fast as I could but I would not make it back to the entrance. I heard the sound of the wrench again, I dared to look back and I saw the thing running towards me on all fours. I could feel myself start to cry, the liquid burning my eyes.

I had to get home. One word kept me going, "Amalie" I said, "Amalie, Amalie". Somehow I reached an exit. I sneaked through the small hole in the barbwire fence. There was no way that the thing was going to fit through the hole. Was there? I carried on running until I couldn't even stand and my legs started to wobble. I must have eventually collapsed on the ground. I only remember waking up and seeing nothing but white. I thought I was dead, I started shivering, then I realised I was covered in at least twelve feet of snow. Wildly, I tried to push the snow off me but I had no strength left. I was going to die, I knew it, but then I felt the snow getting lighter, and lighter. Then I saw daylight, but it was immediately filled by a tall bearded man in a suit. He helped me up and before I could blink he was gone, nowhere to be seen.

I looked down and saw a loaf of bread with a card stuck in it.

OVERDUE NOTICE

Please pay what is owed at the lighthouse library.

Possessed
Mason Purdy

Swinging in the dark alone, alone

No light but the moon

His name echoing in the chain of the swing, in the night's breeze.

    Still no movement.

Worried and scared, feeling the loss, his possessed son.

Alone and cold, feeling himself disappearing.

Gone and possessed, lost to the night

Never to be found, never his.

What to Play
Tippi Wilson

I don't know what I want to play.

The little girl eyed the dolls strewn about the floor.

Princesses…

She picked up one figurine that vaguely resembled Cinderella, silky blue dress and blonde locks.

… or forests. Woods. Little Red Riding Hood.

As usual, her hand fell around Cinderella, hoisting it up off the floor. She had all day, and all night, and could always play the other game later.

Not that she would.

She needs a prince…

Once again, she scanned what was left of the tiny, wooden people; a little boy, etched on smile half faded, a girl, no older than seven. Kind of like her. Lastly, a man, grand blue top and trousers adorning its body. Seemed appropriate for a prince.

This went on for some time, the characters interacting in a clumsy sort of dance and the girl made them 'talk' or 'dance'. That was until her sister came, sitting herself down and plucking the toy she'd wanted to play with next off the floor.

Maybe, when she was four and her sister only three, she would have kicked up a fuss, screaming and crying, yelling at the younger of the two. But now, she just watched, she didn't make a sound. Her sister continued to play, giggling as she did. She hadn't even acknowledged the elder for quite some time.

"Hey Annie." Still the younger didn't listen and continued to conduct her 'story' in the dolls' house.

She knew that soon, 'Annie' would be called for tea, and she wouldn't see her again, not until the next day. Maybe not even then. But she looked forward to it, whenever 'it' may be.

She missed the little things. Like being called for dinner and running along, tripping over and waiting as he sister toddled along trying in vain to catch up. Nothing would be like that again, and she accepted it. Accepted not hearing her mother call her name, nor her father. But she missed it, missed it a lot.

As expected, the soft voice of her mama carried from the kitchen, alerting her little sister. She watched as Annie dropped her doll and stood, taking up a fast and unsteady walk to the kitchen.

There's always tomorrow.

The Vigleno Disease
Deolu Fakorede

I never thought that my wife was ill. She was in tip-top shape; went jogging every night behind our farm. But to be honest I should have noticed her glazed eyes and greying hair. Now the clues seem so obvious. She was always awake before me and in bed after I was fast asleep. She was always down there in the kitchen when I came down to breakfast. Then one day I asked her why she was not taking the kids to school and she told me they were old enough to walk. She had always jogged with them through the forest behind our farm and carried their lunches in her little tartan sack, but not today. That was when I first realised something was wrong.

Why would she stop all of a sudden? Geoffrey drove me to our local doctor but when I described the symptoms, this doctor was as clueless as I was. He lent me his 'Big Encyclopaedia of Diseases', but what my wife had seemed to be in a league of its own; not something you could place under a heading in that big shiny book. This is when I decided to go to Ko-Jin. He is a priest and a man of knowledge, although I'm not sure of what religion or of what science. He barely let me finish my sentence. In his eyes there was only one explanation for this: Vigleno Disease. It spreads fast but kills you slowly from the feet up, taking precisely three years.

Lewis came to say that two of our livestock had been killed in the night by a wolf. This was not a good day. I retired to my library and searched all my history books. The disease was once common and those who suffered were often considered witches and made to suffer until their penultimate day of living, before they were executed. There had been many people trying to solve the Vigleno mystery, but none had succeeded. There was clearly no cure.

That morning I noted how well the children were coping. Perhaps they did not yet understand. I knew I had to go back to Ko-Jin. He had to tell me what to do. I sat with my head in my hands as Geoffrey drove. I ran into the temple, sweating, but he was not there. I asked around but the locals sneered and jerked at the sound of his name. The postman told me of a mysterious man in the remote corner of the village – A mysterious man who was up with the sun every morning, practising mixed martial arts in his brown robes. This had to be him.

I finally found the house at 7pm. The house was old and decrepit. It was about as small as a garden shed. I stumbled down the path and knocked on the door. No answer came. I knocked on the door again, but I was left with no answer. I knocked for a third and final time, much louder now. Then I heard a rustling, I felt a tap on my shoulder. I sprang round and it was Ko-Jin, a wry smile on his face.

"Take this." He said after I had finished explaining my research and my concerns.

It was a little pear-shaped glass bottle filled with a sort of purple ink.

"I thought you said there was no cure." I said.

We exchanged a silence. That Friday the village paper reported the death of my wife from the mysterious and unfortunate Vigleno Disease. They did not mention the purple ink.

Wolf Heart
Charli Eglinton

As he walks towards it, the crowd stare in silence. He considers escaping but he'll just be caught again. Besides, he is willing to walk towards it…after all he's done.

It rang around the empty streets. Birds fled from the trees. A spine chilling scream hit him in the chest. He thundered through the puddles, through the empty streets to where the growing crowd gathered. He pushed his way to the front to recoil in horror. Clara sat, bowed over a body, a body of a child.

"Harvey!" he stammered.

"My son!" she cried. People began to murmur and whisper behind them. A cart clattered down the road, halting beside them. A policeman stepped out and gestured only Clara inside. Henry wanted to call after them but the words wouldn't come out. Instead, tears bubbled up in his throat. He stood rigid watching the distant silhouette become enveloped by the fog. When he entered his mansion, Nicholas, his assistant, greeted him.

"Henry, are you alright?" He glared at him before running upstairs, slamming the laboratory door behind him. Nicholas anxiously combed his fingers through his hair and gulped.

Henry sunk into a chair and sobbed.

"What have I *done*?" he cried. There came a knock at the door.

"Henry…" Nicholas began "what's happened?"

"Go away!" he growled.

"Please let me in, Henry. If there's something wrong maybe I can help…" Henry slowly raised his head.

"No one can help what I have done!" he opened the door. Tears streamed down his face like little rivers dividing into smaller brooks. His breathing was stuttered." My son is dead!" Nicholas' jaw dropped and slowly he raised a hand to his mouth.

"Oh my God! You poor man…" he reassuringly patted Henry on the back.

"I am simple idiot!" he rested his head on Nicholas' shoulder. Silence drowned the room.

"I'm sorry." Nicholas eventually whispered. "What happened?"

"I don't know. I heard a scream and then I find Clara weeping beside Harvey in the middle of the road. I was supposed to take him to school but I let him go by himself." Henry absently looked into space. "Clara trusted me to do it because for one day she had something else to do. I promised her I would but what have I just gone and done? He's been run over and it's my entire fault! She'll never forgive me…" Henry trailed off and broke down into tears once more. Lost for words, Nicholas blankly stared out in front of him-still patting Henry on the back. "Nicholas," he muttered "Could I be by myself now. I need sometime alone."

"Of course. If there's anything I can do…"

"Please," he constrained "Just go." Nicholas crept out of the room, gently closing the door. Henry collapsed his head into his hands.

Henry ran through wet streets following the distant cry of Clara's voice. It echoed from every direction.

"Clara?" he panted. Distressed, Henry staggered down small cobbled streets and roads growing more worried with each step he took. He abruptly stopped to find Clara arched over Harvey. He gasped when he saw a fast carriage hurtle towards them. The horse tried to brake, but skidded with the wet pavements-Clara totally unaware.

"No!" he shrieked.

Henry shot up. He checked around the room to see a desk, shelf after shelf of books, a small table with a white sheet draped over it and a metal door facing him. It was a relief to realize he was still in his laboratory. He smiled to accept that what he witnessed was a dream. A horrible, cruel dream. Henry suddenly noticed he overlooked something in the room. The door was ajar and in front of it stood a young woman with long blonde hair, blazing green eyes and a pale face like a thin white sheet. Henry gulped. "Clara?"

"Henry, I…" she paused before putting her hands to her eyes and started to softly whimper. He stood up and walked over to her. He gently closed his arms around her delicate frame.

"Hey it's alright." He comforted.

"It's not! It's my entire fault!" she cried.

"No it's not…" Clara found her way out of Henry's clasp and stood back.

"You're right. It is not my fault. It's yours! I gave you one instruction: take Harvey to school. But no, you may be a genius when it comes to science but when it comes to common sense you are a FOOL!" He'd never seen Clara like this before.

"But Clara…I had an important experiment I'd been planning for months, years even. I thought Harvey could take himself to school…"

"For God's sake, Henry! You really think your child's life is less worthy than some stupid, pointless science experiment? Henry, wake up! Your son is dead! Besides, your science is wrong, it defies the laws of nature. When you became a scientist, I may have looked happy for you but I couldn't have been less pleased!"

"Science is my life, it's everything I've ever worked towards."

"Fine." Clara began. "I get it. You love it so much; you can have your science! I'll go somewhere where I can get some real sympathy!"

"Clara wait!"

"Goodbye Henry." She said shakily on the verge of crying. As she left, Nicholas entered with a tray of two glasses and a bottle of port. His face confused and bewildered.

"What on earth happened?" he asked. Henry slumped in his chair.

"As if Clara wasn't upset enough already, I managed to send her through the roof! She'll never forgive me! Unless..." Henry sprang up and hastened toward the back of the room where a table sat with a white cloth donned over it.

He whisked it off to reveal a lifeless brown hare stretched out on the table. "Nicholas, our experiment this morning...where I used the serum from the vivificabet plant-located somewhere in the rainforest-to resurrect this rabbit using another one's heart. This is done by injecting the serum into the other one's heart-remember? I wonder if it would work on Harvey..."

"Are you mad? Henry, a rabbit's heart won't be large enough to sustain a boy!"

"No, no." Henry mused "we would need a bigger heart...like the heart of a human. Nicholas, go out into the cemetery and find me a fresh heart!" Nicholas stared at him in disbelief.

"Henry, this is fine on lab animals but human beings?"

"Please, I implore you. It's the only chance I have to win Clara back and bring Harvey back to life." Nicholas reluctantly pulled on a heavy overcoat and headed out. Henry began to prepare his equipment.

Quite some later, Nicholas returned cold and peppered with snow. In his hands he held a wooden box. Inside the box was splattered with blood and in the centre, the heart. Henry made him a hot drink but he didn't say anything. It was as if he was hiding something. "Shall we begin?" he asked. Henry had recovered the body prior to Nicholas' return. They lay the body on the table. Henry looked at the inert boy. He gave it a ghost of a smile. He was about to start the operation, a thin knife balanced in his palm, when Nicholas finally piped up,

"I don't think this is right..."

"Oh?"

" It seems wrong. It goes against the laws of nature. Is it right to bring Harvey back to life? What if it causes Clara more grief? What if something goes wrong?"

"Trust me, I know what I'm doing." Nicholas stood back, regret flickering in his eyes. He picked up the bottle of serum. The operation took all night. Henry finished as the tip of the sun poured into the room like a spilt paint can. He fell back into a chair and found himself in a strange and irrational dream. Henry woke to hear Clara's voice. He couldn't work out what she said or where she was. At first he tried to wave it away until he became aware of the knock at the door.

"Henry?" she called "Are you in there?" He sat motionless in the chair.

"So what if I am, are you going to come back in here and tell me off again?"

"No. I came to say I'm sorry. Will you forgive me?" he smirked and opened the door.

"How could I not forgive you?" he gestured her in. She screamed in horror as Henry turned to see what she witnessed. Harvey lay on the table-in plain sight-with a long red stitch all the way up his chest.

"Please Clara! Don't panic! I will explain."

She watched him tentatively.

"You remember when I went on that trip to the rainforest?"

She nodded.

"Well, I found this plant and when I tested it, I discovered it could resurrect living organisms! So I've transplanted Harvey's heart and now if I add some of the serum…" he picked the bottle up and squeezed a few drops into Harvey's mouth. His fingers tensed and he sat up. Harvey blinked repeatedly and surveyed the room. "Yes! I've done it! It works!"

"Harvey, Is it really you?" Clara asked hesitantly, almost to herself. He sat as still as before. She gulped and hugged him tightly but he wriggled his way out. He met Henry's gaze. There was something about the way he looked at him that was slightly unnerving. His eyes were cold and hollow like frozen water. He turned to Nicholas.

"See, I told you I knew what I was doing!"

She nodded. They both wanted to believe that things could be back to normal.

The following morning, Henry took Harvey to school and saw him safely through the gates. At school, Harvey was oblivious to the rumour of his resurrection. During a lesson, he grew drowsy and fell asleep at the desk. All the other children burst into a wave of laughter. He quickly jerked to find himself encircled by taunts and giggles. He growled nervously and the laughter exploded.

"Harvey thinks he's a dog!" One girl cried. Her name was Amanda Granite. She had long brown plaits, round glasses and her face was dotted with freckles.

"Look! It's dog-boy!" a boy shouted. His name was Marcus Pindell. More and more people began to swarm around Harvey chanting

"Dog-boy! Dog-boy!"

"I'm not a dog!" he roared "You may laugh now but I'll get my own back!"

"You and what army?" Marcus scoffed.

"My army is stronger than all of you put together!" Harvey sat upright and got back to work. Not satisfied with his response, Marcus threw a pen at Harvey's back. He shot up and raced across the classroom. He sprung on Marcus before he could run. Harvey sank his teeth into his arm, penetrating the skin. Marcus shrieked in agony. The teacher was too late to stop him.

"Harvey! Stop! Stop!" she cried. Harvey was suddenly torn from the victim's side by the scruff of his collar. The head teacher stood with disgust on his face.

"Harvey Herlate! What in God's name do you think you are doing? Miss, take Marcus to a first-aider, Harvey come with me." Mr Farenturn paced the room with anger. "How dare you! What were you thinking? You are out of order, boy! Harvey, you were my top student, what happened? I'm going to have to tell your parents. Behaviour like this is unacceptable."

When Henry received the call from Mr. Farenturn, he couldn't believe what he heard.

"Harvey, how could you! I can't understand it…" he gestured him to get out of his sight.

"He used to be an angel…" Clara said. Henry began to feel as if his plan hadn't gone as intended. That night, Harvey snuck out of the window and clambered down the tree. He ran away from the house and towards the village.

When Henry woke Harvey up the next morning, he stared at him before heading downstairs. Henry was about to make his bed when he noticed blood stains dotted around the mattress. He examined them more closely to find torn bits of human flesh mixed with blood. Perhaps he cut himself? It seemed the most logical answer at the time. Henry sat down at the table with his newspaper. The headline stated in bold:

Mysterious Murderer

'Marcus Pindell and Amanda Granite were murdered last night in their homes in Purbeck Hills. The children's bodies were not found but their beds were sodden with blood. Police presume it was a wild animal that may have escaped from a private residence. You are well warned to look out for anything of that sort.'

Henry threw the paper on the table and hurried downstairs. He knocked on the door of Nicholas' office.

"Nicholas are you in there?"

"What is it ,Henry? You look distressed." he rose from his chair.

"You did get me the heart of a human, didn't you?"

"Not exactly…" he muttered.

"What do you mean 'not exactly'?" Henry demanded.

"Oh I can't hide it any longer! All the bodies in the

cemetery were just bones and no flesh with no heart. So I… shot a wolf…" Henry gasped in realization as everything fitted into place. The bite, the cold stare, the flesh and blood on the bed.

"Then that means…oh no!" Henry made for the door but Nicholas blocked his path.

"What does it mean?"

"It means that Harvey is the killer!"

"How can you be sure?"

"Because the two children that were killed were the ones taunting him at school!" Henry bolted out of the room and up the stairs. He saw Clara walking away from the mansion, towards the village. He needed to tell her his discovery but first Henry needed to make sure Harvey was kept away from trouble. He locked him in his room and sprinted after Clara. Henry finally caught up with her and breathlessly told her what he found. "And that's why we have to get back…before…it's too la-" There came a terrible cry from the mansion. They rushed back as fast as they could. The door was wide open and lying on the floor was Nicholas. He lay face down in a pool of blood. Panting rapidly stood Harvey just behind him. Harvey's face was filled with rage as red droplets trickled down his mouth. "What have you done?" Henry stammered.

"Nicholas!" Clara screamed and ran out of the door.

"Why did you do it? And *how* did you do it? I locked

you in your room!"

"You locked the door but not the window." Harvey mused. "I did it because *he* killed me. I was the alpha wolf in my pack and he shot *me...*"

"This has to stop." Henry drew a revolver from his pocket and took aim. He rested his finger on the trigger. His hand trembled. He couldn't shoot his *own* son! Harvey saw his intention and pounced on Henry. He hurtled backwards, skidding across the tiles. Henry forced himself to his knees and looked around the room. The boy had gone. He checked again in confusion before noticing that he was behind him. Harvey jumped on Henry and he tried to throw him off but he still clung on. He clawed at Henry's face with his nails. Henry shrieked in pain, desperately trying to fight him off. He moved away from Henry's face and pierced his teeth into his leg. He flung Harvey off in a delirious panic and skidded along the floor. He hit the wall with great force. Before he had chance to recover, Henry pulled the trigger. Harvey's eyes widened before he fell to the ground. Everything went silent. The only sound to be heard was Henry's fast breathing and the cold sound of dripping blood from Harvey's chest. He limped over to Nicholas.

"What have I done? You were right, I never should've messed with nature! What have I done?"

And so he; I, Henry Herlate walk towards the gallows

for the murder of Harvey Herlate. Within a matter of minutes I will no longer be in pain and I will no longer be in debt.

Selling Your Soul

James Jones

There was once a village in the middle of the forest. Now there is nothing there because all the villagers died harsh natural deaths.

It all started when a man walked into the village. He was good at everything. He wanted to bring technology to the village but the people didn't want this to happen, so they plotted to kill him. The strange man knew what they were up to.

So he built a machine to consult with the underworld. The earth in front of him was cut in two faster than any plough could cut it. Suddenly, a red demon appeared from the soil. The man knelt and measured the demon then shook his hand.

He returned to the village with faces of enemies surrounding him. He told them he was sorry he could no longer stay any longer because he had a date with a demon, they laughed. As thanks for letting him into their town he said he would leave them a gift. A bottle of red wine, a slice of bread and a toy box, that made a little bulb come on when you turned the handle, for the littlest boy in the village.

Nobody thought of the man again. He was no longer there and so no longer remembered, but neither were the villagers.

The demon had struck on the first date. A glass of red wine and a slice of bread. Now where the village lies, there's nothing left but a veil of poison in the air and an old grey toy factory.

The Birch Tree
Eve Dobel

It all began when I was visiting my Nan's grave. As I stood there the familiar smell of a old smoke brushed past my nose. As I looked around I became sure that nothing was there; no one was there, except a lonely old birch tree with a sharp twig pointing at me. I said goodbye to my Nan and walked home.

I was having a cup of hot chocolate when I realised that the sky had turned dark. The dark grey clouds blocked the sun, which cast a large shadow over the town. I leaned back, strangely enjoying the storm, by I felt something itch my back. I tried to readjust but whatever it was, scratched me. I took my jumper off. There was a twig attached to it, a birch twig.

I lay in bed thinking of all the times I spent with my Nan. Like how she made the best apple and rhubarb pies, making the delicious pastry with her old frail hands. My daydream carried to a rattling noise downstairs. I thought it was her, but then I remembered. It must have been a mouse. Why couldn't she at least have died peacefully in her sleep?

As I turned the telly on, the breaking news burst onto the screen like a rectangular firework. They said: "... John Birch, arrested for manslaughter, has escaped while on parole...." My eyes were fixed on the screen. I recognised something. They showed a picture of a scruffy muscular man with a scar above his right eye. It seemed to silly to think that it was his name that made me feel unsettled. I couldn't quite put my finger on what I was missing here. My hands were shaking. I decided to go to the local shop so I could get some fresh air. I would not have been able to sleep and when I did sleep, I would sleep until lunchtime and need food. It seemed like all the birch trees had rustled their leaves at me, desperate to tell me something. Like the wind had stolen their voices. I walked on. Everyone who walked past me looked at me and whispered. Did everyone else know something I didn't? Was there something in my hair or on my skirt? It was like they were surprised I was out. What had happened that I wasn't to know about? I asked a lady who was walking by: "excuse me…" but before I could say anymore she had run off. It was like I had a disease they didn't want to catch. Maybe I did have a disease. I felt alone. I don't know for how long I had been locking myself away but now was different and I had decided I was going to face the world even if I had to do it on my own. I heard my Nan's voice saying:

"Never run away from darkness, as you don't know when there could be a light within reach."

I got home ten minutes later, I suddenly felt really dizzy. I went upstairs to lie down. I felt a presence. Then I heard a noise. I quietly put on my dressing gown. I didn't know what would frighten me more: if there was someone there, or if there was no-one. Trying to make the least noise possible, I looked down the stairs. I couldn't see. I felt the for the birch twig in my pocket and picket up the phone.

"Hello inspector," I said. "I'm ready to talk. I think I know who killed my grandmother."

Love Created Us
Joeliza Campos

SKYLAR

Burning. Screaming. Dying. ALL GONE! The world was rushing past me like a hail stone striking a window. I was a window. Everything was taking turns to strike me, one after another. I couldn't see through myself. It would have been better if I could not see at all. Speaking? Pointless! Living?

What should I have done with my life? Come on, tell me! I needed help, and no one was there to support me. What was the point in living when the part of me that stuck me together was gone?

I had felt complete. I had felt secure. He had been my frame. But he was gone - murdered! And guess who killed him.

KANE

"Kane? Are you awake?" my God-mother called from two floors below.

"Yes Sandra!" I shouted down.

"Well there is someone on the phone for you! They say it is urgent!"

This was the normal waking up routine. Sandra would shout

up "are you awake", and I would shout down "yes I am!" There was always something loud and urgent in this house.

My mother died when I was born and my father died when I was twelve, during a battle against Ophion -god of the Depths. My brother also died, from a heart defect. My childhood was tough, but I still lived through every day of it.

After my father died, I inherited the title. I came to live in the land of the Gods with my godmother. My parents used to be Free Gods, they went to live in the land of humans to be free. However when my parents died, the Free Gods became quiet. They just lived their normal lives in the land of humans, pretending to be human themselves. One thing that was always on my mind was that Astor (KING of the GODS) wanted me to marry his daughter, Ena, she was very beautiful but I just was not interested. I wanted to be able to say "I have fallen in love" before marrying someone.

SKYLAR

I got to the top of the stairs of the principal's office. He hated having meetings with people that were late. I knocked on the door. There was a faint answer, so I entered.

I found myself standing alone in a large, dingy room. There

was a large table in the centre, with nothing on it but a nearly burnt out candle. I always hated going to the principal's office. He always freaked me out. But I must say almost everything freaked me out in those days.

The darkness in the room seemed heavy enough to put out its solitary flickering light. There was a cloak hanging on one of the chairs, casting a shadow on the wall that seemed like the head of an old man with a crooked nose. This shadow, in the flickering candle light, was quivering, and seemed almost like that old man was nodding to me.

As I concentrated on this shadow, with all my powers, I could feel some sort of presence behind me. This reminded of one of the positions I was in back at home (land of the Gods). No one was meant to know that I was a descendent of a goddess. If it got out, I would be in massive trouble! I didn't exactly know why but before mother died she said that it was something to do with one of our ancestors disturbing the humans.

Suddenly I snapped out of my daydream and realized that I was clinging onto the cloak. I saw from the corner of my eye, a shadow cross one of the paintings on the light grey wall. I went to inspect it. As I walked up to the painting, I heard a noise. It sounded like the heavy tread of a man. I didn't have the courage to turn round.

"Who are you?" I faltered. My hands were quivering along

with the rest of my body. I clenched my gut and turned round.

I asked again "who are you?" The person just laughed coldly. It was a man. His face was hidden by the shadows but the candle dimly lit up his profile. With an evil leer on his face, he moved towards me. Spontaneously, I moved backwards. A thought came to my mind to run, but I knew that that was unwise; partly because I was sure he could outrun me.

I drew to a dead halt when my back hit the wall. I was cornered. With wild eyes and a heavily pounding heart, I stared back at him helplessly. I could not tell, even slightly, who he was; his face was shrouded in darkness. He advanced on me in deliberate slow strides.

Now he was standing before me, his face only a few inches away from mine. Only then could I fully make of his shape. He was a well built young man with broad shoulders, oval jaws, and dark eyes that bore desirously into me. But no, I had read that look wrong. My thoughts turned back to fear. He thrust his hand, suddenly, into his pocket revealing a knife. He pinned me against the wall with his muscular arm and placed the cold blade against my throat.

KANE

I woke up at dawn, even though I hadn't fallen asleep until four.

I lay in bed staring at the faded grey peeling wallpaper, tracing the little line of cracks with my eyes. Today was meant to be the biggest day of my life. I was to kill the goddess of love.

I rolled over and crinkled my nose. She was probably old; like the goddesses of love in the picture books in the old library. I might have been the god of war but books and general knowledge were not my strong point. I decided to stop thinking about it.

I threw my feet over the side of the bed and tiptoed across the worn hardwood floors, trying to avoid the floorboards that I knew would creak. I threw on some dark clothes; Astor had taught me to blend in with the darkness of the room. I knew that I was to go to the land of the humans, but I didn't know where in planet earth I would go. I left the room with the heavy heart of a murderer.

Periwinkle sunshine poured in through the tiny octagonal window at the end of the hall. It cast shadows off the ceiling beams and doorknobs that dappled the ground in light, like a forest floor.

I took one glance at the clock and knew that I needed to do things quickly. So I ran down the stairs. I flung the door open, letting it slam into the wall behind it and stepped out just in time, before it slammed shut again. Sprinting forwards I leapt through the air skipping the steps that lead from the house to the ground.

I got to the deserted train station on time to meet Astor'
assistant waiting with my knife and my ticket. I then boarded the
stationary train and went to find a seat, waiting for the engine to
start running before I could allow myself to breathe.

SKYLAR

I didn't know what else to do but to stare into his eyes. I could
feel the blush and a surprising scream coming up. He finally
spoke.

"Don't scream, I know who you are!" he said in a low voice.
"You are the goddess of love, Skylar. I am the god of war, Kane;
sent to earth by Astor (king of the Gods) to kill you."

I knew that if I didn't do something fast my life would end.
So I said:

"Yes I know who you are!" I took a pause to stare into his
eyes. "You are meant to be getting married to Astor' daughter.
Her name is Ena." I could feel the stern grip loosening from my
chest. He removed the knife from my neck. The boy turned
away. I could breathe. I heard his breath catch.

"Maybe I *should* just slit your throat. The blood would stain
the blade and I could say to Astor that I killed you." He paused

and turned round to look me in the eye. He had some sort of abnormal shine in his eye, "Or I could just kill you now in one smooth incision. But first let me see you in the candle light. I stepped forward. His facial expressions changed completely - or was it the shadows? Usually I could read people's facial expressions. However, he was different. I couldn't do it.

"Please don't!" I cried. "Can't you tell Astor that you couldn't kill me?" Again his face changed and he looked up at me. I carried on. "That way it would be easier for both of us."

"You don't understand! He doesn't except 'no' It always has to be a 'yes'. You have no idea what he can do to you. I have no choice but to kill you!"

All that I remember is Kane lunging forward with his knife, my body went numb then everything became dark.

KANE

I could not believe what I had done. Not just to any girl. I hurt a girl that had illuminated my dreams so many days ago - a girl I now knew I had to love. I thought that she was going to be an old lady but she was beautiful! She had burning blue eyes! Skylar was the most beautiful name. These thoughts spun from my head like the side-plait of her long blonde hair. I loved her. I wanted her. I needed her. NOW!

I did it for the masters own sake. But I had had enough of being his slave. If he wanted to do something he would have to do it himself because I was quitting. It was time for the bird to leave the nest. I would move to planet earth. I would declare WAR! I knew what my father would have said about it, he would support me. It was time to fight.

As I was approaching the station I grew more and more confident. I had everything planned. The train came to a noisy halt, the doors swung open and I stepped out.

SKYLAR

I woke up. Was it a dream? What had happened? I tried to move but was met by a horrible pain through my body! I just moved my head. Aunt Bella was sitting by my bed, when she saw me meet her gaze, her eyes lit up and she opened her mouth in surprise.

"Sky, you're alive! We thought we'd never see you open your eyes again! We found you alone with a dagger rooted in your hip! Your side was leaking blood, so we rushed you home as quickly as we could. Rest now. Oh and this letter came, it's for you but you need to get some sleep first."

68

"I will." I whispered quietly. She left the room closing the door gently behind her. I turned my attention to my un-opened letter. A slight thrill of excitement came over me.

Dearest Skylar,

This is Kane. I don't know if you remember me but we were in your Principal's office and I tried to kill you. Words cannot express how much I regret doing it. Please forgive me.

I decided to lay off the deal with Astor and I am coming to live on Earth as I declared war on him - it's kind of my thing! I am deeply sorry, and wondered if you have the courage to join me, we can fight Astor together. Please, I beg you to join me.

Before I met you, I had given up on ever finding my soul mate; the one person who could set my heart on with just one look. You have touched me deeply like no one else. The feelings are so very difficult to express, if you could only understand my condition. Today I have gathered the guts to put forth my love before you whether you accept it or not. My love for you will only rise. Please don't get me wrong. I just wanted you to know how I feel about you.

Yours sincerely

Kane

I stared absently at the paper. I didn't know what to do. It turns out that the goddess of love has fallen in love herself with her born nemesis and assassin and apparently being the goddess of love, she should know what to do. I had no idea what to do.

As I was wondering about all of this, there was a knock on the door. It was Selene my servant- although we were always very close.

"There is a gentleman at the door that wants to see you. He won't say his name. Should I tell him that you don't want to see anyone at the moment?"

"No. Tell him to come up. But before he does, could you help me brush my hair and could you braid it like you used to do?" she didn't say anything, she just did my hair and went down stairs to tell the visitor to come up.

I decided to pretend I was asleep and so I closed my eyes and accidently drifted off.

KANE

She was asleep when I entered the room. She looked unchanged from the image I held in my imagination. Even her hair was the same. She was such an angel sleeping, I dared not wake her and so I sat on the armchair by her bed. I caressed her pale, thin fingers gently as I waited for her to wake.

When she finally woke up, she didn't realise who was there holding her hand. After a few seconds, she came to her senses and looked me in the eye. Love at second sight. Slowly, with my other hand I started to stroke her head, hair going through my fingers as if honey.

"Why did you do that?" she asked. I didn't know what she meant. Why did I declare war or why did I try to kill her?

"Declare war or try to kill you?"

"Both really, and more." She laughed faintly.

"Well I declared war because I have had enough of being bossed around by Astor. I want independence. I am strong and ready. And I did it so that I could come and find you. I found your address and decided to send you a letter did you..."

"Get it? Yes. I loved that letter. I will join you as long as you help me learn how to walk again. And last of all..." she paused. "I could love you too but I am not ready to be with you until the battle is over. I need to concentrate."

A SONG ON THE WIND

Kane stayed with Skylar. He helped her get fit and strong for the battle ahead. Every day Skylar got fitter, stronger, and wiser with the help of her best friend but not yet boyfriend. As well as training with each other the two created an amazing bond.

They spent the next year training, bonding and loving. They both loved each other more than the muses could imagine. The day of the battle was getting closer and closer and closer each day.

The sun appeared behind the spires of her home. The year had passed.

SKYLAR

"You know I feel confident that you are going to be an amazing fighter on that battle field."

"Kane", I breathed, my head falling on his chest, "I love you."

"You don't need to say it; I can see it in your eyes." He wrapped his arms around me and kissed my forehead. I put my hand in his, stood up and pulled him up with me.

I knew that for us to both be happy together we had to stay together forever in an official bond. Kane had been patient and I loved him dearly for that. I decided to make the first move. "You know I said I didn't want to have a relationship until after the battle? Well I have changed my mind."

He leaned on me. He pushed aside a strand of hair that was in front of my face behind my ear and lowered his hand to behind my neck. I was still waiting for an answer. He pulled me to him and kissed me. I guess that was it.

It lasted for a long time. I felt like I had bats in my mouth. When we eventually stopped he picked me up and carried me into the house. I felt so happy! It felt like nothing could make me unhappy. We both walked up the stairs and we stopped at my room. He said:

"You should get some sleep. We have a big day tomorrow." The light bared his expression. He had dark grey eyes that shone like the moon, and light brown hair. I nodded obediently. He kissed me again and hugged me before disappearing into the darkness of the next set of stairs. I entered my bedroom feeling happy. I changed into my Pajamas and slipped into bed. Once my head hit the pillow I fell asleep dreaming only of him.

KANE

I woke up at dawn, feeling ecstatic. Last night was the best night I ever had. Skylar was to be under my protection today, even though she was amazingly strong. If I have to die for her, today was the day.

I threw my feet across the side of the bed. Now it was time to wake Skylar up, and I knew just how to do it. I tiptoed down the stairs to her bedroom. I paused, hand wrapped around the doorknob.

ONE, TWO, THREE.

I flung the door open, letting it slam into the wall behind it. I sprinted forward, leaping through the air at the very last moment and pounced on Skylar in her enormous bed. She screamed and leaped up. Once she realised it was me she sunk into her bed again.

"Oh, it's you, Kane. You frightened me! What time is it?"

"Six in the morning!"

"What, already?" she asked with a worried tone in her voice. She then sat up. I kissed her and got off the bed.

"Hurry we only have one hour to get to the station where everyone will meet us. And remember the outfit." She did her normal obedient nod and walked into the bathroom.

We all decided to wear black. The women would wear tight black shiny tops and shiny black leggings with their own traditional make up. Each goddess had a different hair style and make up style. The men were to wear black T-shirts and black jeans with a leather jacket.

I ran up the stairs to go and get changed. Once I finished, I got my weapon and ran back down the stairs to see my beautiful girl dressed and ready leaning against the wall. She looked amazing. She had her hair out brushed looking like silk. Her make up all black. She was now the goddess of love that will not let anyone get in her way. She went from an immature nineteen year old to an adult in this past year. I was so proud of her.

SKYLAR

He looked so handsome. The fighter is going to win the battle with me. We were both ready. I had to say goodbye to my godmother because I wasn't going to live here anymore. Kane and I decided to live in the land of gods. It was so hard.

"Make sure you call me when the battle is over. And good luck my baby." I knew I couldn't cry otherwise I would smudge the makeup that Selene did for me the last time.

"I promise. And I will miss you." We all said bye to each other and Kane and I got into the taxi that would take us to the train station.

We got there in no time at all. We got out of the taxi with our hands interlocked. I had never seen so many people wearing the same things!

They all had their fighting faces on. Time to get them back! Kane and I lead the pack into the train. The train today would be packed. We were still going to meet many more people in the land of gods.

KANE

We got there at eleven in the morning. We were only half an hour away from the battle field. I felt my stomach go weird. I needed to protect Skylar. That would mean I'd have to give anything to keep her safe, including my life. She had powers that could kill many strong people. I have the magical sword that can fight well and everyone else has their own powers. Together we made a strong team.

From the station we all entered the forest. On the other side the people of Astor would be waiting for us. Skylar and I lead the team towards them.

"Kane I love you!" she said.

"Don't do that! You're not going to die, ok! I love you too." I answer. I grabbed hold of her. We all looked at one another. We knew we were going to have to win this no matter what.

Skylar quickened her pace. She was angry and when she was angry you couldn't get in her way. She had a serious look on her face. We got to the end of the forest and we started to see the opposing team.

"You all know what to do; we have been training hard for this. So let's go. ONE, TWO, *THREE*... Charge!" I shouted at the top of my voice. Skylar and I ran side by side. She pulled out her bow and arrow and I pulled out my sword. The battle began.

Skylar shot down every single person unlucky enough to get into her range. She seemed to have an endless supply of the arrows. I fought ferociously with my sword. Everything shot up in flames. People were screaming. No matter how many times I would cut someone, the sword was sharp and had no blood stain.

We carried on fighting for five long hours, until I lost sight of Skylar. I started to look for her but ended up finding Astor. This was my battle...

SKYLAR

I was so tired. I needed to rest but I just couldn't. I had to carry on. Everything was literally on fire. People were screaming. I stopped fighting and started to dodge the people to look for Kane. I eventually found him fighting Astor, both with blood pouring down their faces. They seemed to be having a conversation at the same time as fighting. I had to stop them.

Kane was getting knocked down. I had to get there. The problem is they were on the other side of the battle field. So I ran faster than I ever had before. I dodged.

I shoved.

I shot.

I was almost there.

I got there just as Astor was finishing with Kane.

"Oi. Astor." I called.

He stood up. Just as he looked at me I shot him, right in his heart. I just carried on shooting until he fell with a surprised look on his face. However, he still had the spear in his hand. With one last aim he threw the spear in my direction, but now Kane was hugging me. The spear hit him in the middle of his back. He almost screamed. Kane fell to the ground.

I screamed.

"NO!" Everyone stopped. I didn't know what to do. People tried to help but I just screamed at them. I was cradling him begging a god to give him one more chance. Just as I was about to give up, he opened his eyes.

He too was crying. We both knew he wasn't going to make it. Slowly one by one the people started to fall to their knees. Slowly everyone realised that there was no point in fighting. Slowly everyone realised who their real king was. Astor was dead. But Kane was dying! Why had I not made Astor drop the spear, why had I let Kane hug me? I killed him.

"I love you Skylar! Just don't forget me! I saved you and you should be happy that you're not dying!" He turned to everyone. "You know who your king is. And you know who your queen is." He looked me in the eye. "Just remember me! And what the free people did to save you. Be friends. Love your neighbour. I love you all." With all his energy, he looked at me. "I love you!"

"I love you too." I said. He took one last breath and closed his eyes. Everyone went silent.

Burning. Screaming. Killing. ALL GONE! The world was rushing past me like a hail stone striking a window.

I take an arrow from my sheath. The poison will kill me in seconds. I stand up and look around. The moon is red. The people on the battlefield stood too and turned to face me. They raised their guns, their swords, their spears. I counted down.

"ONE." We were ready. "TWO" We took a breath. "THREE"

True love never dies.

Crow
i. Anya Whitman

The wind was howling and the moon glistened within the clouds. Beyond the trees was a small, cramped cottage. There lived a girl called Melissa. Melissa was a beautiful young girl, who had shiny brown eyes. All Melissa ever wanted was a handsome young man to share her life with.

The next day she was strolling through the woods back home after a hard working day. She was taking interest in the bark of the trees which towered above her, when a flock of formidable black crows swirled around her. Endless feelings were circling around her head, she started running like she had never run before. She stumbled and fell, the tumble had mutilated her and blood started dripping. It was like dark red rubies had exploded from a safe. The crows vanished…

She pulled herself up. Quickly, she walked back home, but saw a small piece of skin on her doorstep. Using a brightly coloured leaf she nudges it off. The door creaked open. She wondered into the kitchen to make dinner. Picking up a bowl she saw a shiny black feather lying in the centre. Startled, she ran into the living room. Slime, like thick saliva, was dripping everywhere, from the chair to the telly. Climbing the stairs she ran to bed and slithered under her duvet. After some time she reached for the light, but instead grabbed a crow! Keeping her eyes fixed on the crow she saw a golden shape in its mouth. Melissa tried to catch it with both hands, but failed. It flew away, out of the window and into the sparkling night sky. She cries out,

"It stole my grandmother's broach"

But no one hears her.

The next day, Melissa got up bright and early; she was going to find that crow. It was probably rummaging through houses up and down the street and dropping all its look in its nest. She packed her bags with the precious belongings and stepped outside. Last night she managed to see that the crow was heading for the East of the Mills. Melissa started to wonder in that direction, whistling as she went and breathing in the cool green from the mountains all around her village. Everywhere she looked she seemed to see the same black feathers as she saw the night before. Would she know which was the right one? She surely would. Melissa headed for the village where business was starting. The butcher was setting up his stall, the banker was marching to the bank.

As the next few hours passed she was getting weary. Melissa's head was overflowing with questions. Should she give up? What's the point? Should she carry on? It was driving her insane. Madness took over her. Ripping bushes, banging on every door she saw, she ended up lying exhausted on a dark emerald green surface. Villagers started to come out to find what all the noise was. They all gather around Melissa as she lay there not moving. Melissa's chest starts to slow down. Her dread grows as she does not think she will be able to get up. A small, slick black animal appeared with a hint of gold. Flying through the tall, autumn trees it landed on her chest. Focusing as hard as she could she can see her grandmother's broach dangling from its mouth. Slowly, the crow starts to sink down, to melt into her. Seconds later, the villagers see her beautiful eyes gently shut. The broach lies there, untouched, on her chest, covered in the faintest slime. Dust and leaves hover over her as she fades away in the autumn sky.

---

ii. Charlotte Cubitt

The Gothic princess entered the graveyard
And there stood the black crow
There she stared with pale skin scarred
Within an instant, the black crow began to grow
The pale man with silver eyes
Black hair that hit the floor
Had knelt and made her white hand rise
Her ashen hair unveiled no more
Princesses's innocence floods out
She feels his evil gaze fill her
Red rose lips pout, a bout of doubt
Within her, thoughts began to blur
Then the mist opened and clear light shone
Reflecting on the silver sword
Without a word the man was gone
This sixth or seventh noble lord
Blood dripped away, her heart moved on
She laughed but once and called the crows
Who swooped by her, one per gravestone
They formed her cloak, she took her pose
Her eyes turned black, she was alone
She disappeared into the heavenly glow

iii. *Tippi Wilson*

Why? Why was it that, when I finally felt like I was accepted into a school, I had to see it? Did someone somewhere hate me? I've definitely had my fair share of bad luck. I used to believe we each had the same amount of luck in a lifetime, but I am living evidence that that is not true. I mean, what is luck? No, I don't believe in luck anymore. And this is why:

My second week of my *fourth* school. In 2 years. I'd feared it. But I put it off. Don't make yourself feel bad when there's no need to, I told myself. Putting on my headphones, I turned the music up loud so I wouldn't have to think. Flicking through the screen, I finally settled on some motionless in white. Oh, yeah. That's another thing... The reason I've had to move schools 3 times is because of bullying. It got bad, really bad. And the reason? The music I liked, the way I dressed. I didn't realise it was a sin, but apparently to them, it is. Anyway, that's all behind me. The people at this school like me. I've got friends. Good friends.

I lurched backwards as I reached the edge of the forest. I don't know why, but this place sends shivers down my spine. The dark, twisted trees mock you as you walk through. They block out the sun, even in the middle of the day. Just get through, I thought. Then I'll be able to see Alexandaq and Alice. Alice had her fair share of bad happenings herself. Her mum died when she was six.

Quickening my step, I tried not to look at the trees, the dark sky, and…the crow. No…It couldn't be…no, don't be silly. That could be any old crow. There are crows everywhere in America. Especially in forests! But somewhere deep down, I knew it was the first sign. Focus on getting out. It was just a crow! According to the kids from my own school, I'm meant to be 'macabre' and 'dark' and whatever, so why not live up to it? Crows are big in horror films, are they not? But this isn't a horror film. This is MY life; this is real. And that's when I saw, no, heard it. I felt the cold creep up on me, freezing my insides, chilling my bones. Then it whispered in that nasty, rattling voice I feared so much 'Sammi… Sammi… listen… Alice… car… car crash' It whispered, next to my ear. No this can't be happening. It just can't. Not again. I thought if we moved, again, it would stop. They wouldn't follow me here. I thought the ghosts, the deceased, or as I now know them, death prophets had had enough of me. They tell me when someone is about to die. It's a curse, I tell you! When will it stop?!

Usually, they tell me of someone irrelevant about to die. A random nobody; never someone I know. I dreaded this day, and now it's here, I don't know what to do. But. Wait. There was something different about this one. It told me, I think, *how* my friend was going to die. What's more it was still there. Could it…could it tell me how to save her? I pleaded, begged 'Help me, help me! How can I prevent it? I'll do anything!' It extended a long, shrived feather. Clasped beneath it was a letter. On the front was written 'To loved ones' and an address. 'Take this…take this…stop from… taking car journey…friend saved…Help me, I will help' and with that, it disappeared. I looked at the address. I knew what to do. I ran, back the way I'd come.

A year later I looked up at the all too familiar heavy, iron gates. A bunch of flowers in my hand, the other curled in a loose fist. I took a step onto the hard gravel road. Most people found this place creepy, especially at night. I didn't. I liked it, here I could relax, pretend she was still here. I know I shouldn't fool myself, but it helped. People must think I'm mad when I talk to the grave. Mind you, not many people came here so I could more or less have a little time for myself. I looked at the still-fresh epitaph written across a slab of cold, grey stone. I stared the wilted flowers that were scattered across the slight mound of earth, barely visible. I picked up the wilted flowers, replacing them with a fresh bunch. 'Alice. Alice I miss you. We all miss you. I hope you're happy wherever you are… I know you're with your mum now. I` Know you're happy' I dropped the last flower on her grave and walked away.

---

iv. Madeleine Sturgeon-Kell

I ran, that is all I did. Well, I didn't want to go back to that manic place. It was crazy back at home. It was as if something had taken over the whole village. Anyway, I just wanted to get away from that place.

Just entering the mountain range as the sun was setting, it was beautiful, but I couldn't enjoy the view for long. I had to get away (fast) from the threat of death; from the threat of my own parents.

Basically, I had just come back from school and I was playing Catch the Coal with my little brother Tommy and I heard the crows pecking on the bird feeder so I went to get some bird food. As I left the room my mum arrived home from work. She didn't say anything so I just tried to avoid her. My mum had always been odd. Dad was the same. When we ate dinner mum was talking about ghosts and all that rubbish.

Then, she started acting like a bird: jerking her shoulders and her arms up and down, twitching her head from side to side, making guttural high pitched squawks. Obviously, she was ill so I tried to take her up to bed but she tried to bite me and I ran away. I might have been eaten by my own mother.

Then, I'm walking up The Mountain and I see a grass roofed hut on the ridge. I think, "I should see if I can stay there for the night". As I approach the hut, I see a man sitting in front of the fire. Around him lay shelves of bottles and jars and complicated equipment like in the science lab at school. I never really paid attention at school because it was so boring. There were always more pressing matters to try and deal with. When I knock on the door it creaks open and a small decrepit face peers through the gap. He looks like the world has given up on him. He looks like the feeling is mutual. He invites me in and asks me to address him as Klaus. He says I could sleep on the fur skin rug in an empty room on the side of the hut. He asks me why I came and I tell him about the whole experience of my mum acting like a feral crow. He sighs.

Klaus explained that a similar thing happened to his childhood sweetheart. He doesn't offer many details and I don't want to ask. I think that this must be why he lives on the border of the village all alone. Apparently, he saw a crow hopping around his sweetheart's ankles before she went mad. My mind was buzzing with terrifying thoughts of dancing crows ruining the lives of the people of this village. Did the crows attack them? Or were the crow possessing people? I asked Klaus. He said he was toying with the idea for years but he has now just given up on all of it. He is too old to walk down the mountain to warn the villagers.

Next day, I had felt well rested and was getting ready to cross the border when Klaus slipped into my room. He was muttering about something. Something along the lines of someone finally believing him but I was too busy getting ready. I should really listen to other people but the information often just washes by. I might have understood more about all of this if I'd heard the beginning of Klaus's speech. Instead, I turned around just in time to hear "You must therefore die!" A thought flashed through my mind: Klaus, the only person I felt I could trust, was possessed by crows and I was the only person left, perhaps. So I just jumped through the window letting shards of glass scatter over the frosty alpine grass. I ran, that is all I did…

Night
Avneet Chahal

Walking through the forest trees,
    I breathe deeply,
    Through the dark black foggy night,
    I look up to the sky,
    I see the bright moon,
    I see my true light,
    Running swiftly through the moons rays,
    I remember my past,
    But think of that day,
    I was where I am right now… happy,
    Until a presence appeared and took my neck,
    And now I am what I am,
    A human by day,
    A wolf by night.

Murmurs
Ellen Teesdale

It was just another boring day for Jess Bassar. She woke up at 6:00 in the morning, brushed her hair and did her makeup, ate breakfast and left the small apartment. The apartment was awful and she hated it. The faded white paint was now peeling and the threadbare carpet was so dirty that you wouldn't have been able to make out the pattern even if you were the creator. Her room also had an eerie feel about it. When she was sleeping she would wake up suddenly, swearing that she had heard banging! She didn't have any neighbours to be banging on the wall. It was unnerving. As she walked through the dark streets of Limplie, she could smell the bin lorry before she saw it. Her area was alright really. Yes there was graffiti and yes there were the occasional stabbings and yes there was an unsafe "feel" about the place but it was home and that was how she thought of it. This was her home - this was where she lived.

She swiped her card and opened her office door and was greeted by her fellow workers. Then she spotted her – Lynette, her best friend. Lynette would tell Jess she was the only one who didn't treat her differently. Lynette went missing six years ago but when she was found, she was never the same. She had been tortured so badly that she had a seizure. Jess didn't treat her with over the top kindness. Jess treated Lynette with care and love just like she treated her family and her other friends. They greeted each other with a hug and got down to work. They were the editors of 'The Shut-Up and Read' magazine and they both enjoyed reading the funny comments and finding about facts about the other people in this world. When they were together they felt immortal. Wait! What was that? Jess looked up. "Did you hear that? That Bang!" she said.

"Ummmmm… No." Lynette said.

Jess went back to her work but that noise was still on her mind. It sounded just like the ones that she heard almost every night. She could have been sure that she heard a bang. Still unsure of what to do she tried to put it to the back of her mind but… but… it kept her thinking. Throughout the day her body was in the office but her mind was elsewhere.

Lynette sat down. The plate in front of her was piled high with mashed potato and cheese. It had been a long day at work, made longer by Jess's interminable daydreaming… That 'noise'. Why was it such a big deal? No one else had heard it… so why was it such a big deal?

Jess tucked the duvet around her and snuggled down. She felt clean and calm after her shower. There was still a faint smell of artificial forest flowers. She felt warm and her eyelids were becoming heavy and she felt completely… BANG! She jumped up with a start. There it was again. That noise. She clenched her fists so hard that her knuckles turned white and she felt like her skin was going to rip down her hand. Was she just imagining things? Maybe she needed to see a therapist? She got back into bed and positioned herself to fall asleep again. Her body was tired but her mind was wide awake.

Music came blaring through the speakers, waking Jess up. She ate her breakfast and listened to the rain outside. She walked down the alleyway and through the dark streets. The BANG. It was still on her mind. Why was she still thinking about it? It was just a dream. When she got to the office she heard a small gasp and turned to look for the source. Lynette. Why had she gasped? Lynette ushered Jess in to the bathroom and turned Jess so that Jess was facing the mirror. "What happened?" asked Lynette. "You look awful when you don't wear makeup. Everyone can see your old acne scars and why haven't you brushed you hair?" Jess just stood there gawping at her reflection. Her raven black hair was all tangled up and her face was actually dirty. "Here, use mine." Lynette held up a bag filled to the brim with toiletries. Jess took the bag gratefully but when she tried to make herself look presentable, her hand shook with nerves. What? "Here, let me." Lynette offered. Jess accepted gratefully. The two girls were busying themselves so much that they didn't notice the hobbling man in the street – nor did they hear his banging.

"Well, Press Day tomorrow!" said Jess. "Yeah, Bye!" said

Lynette, "See you tomorrow."

"Yeah, see you." replied Jess. The hobbling man smirked to himself thinking that the girls' next meeting might not be quite so soon.

Lynette woke with a start. She had heard something; not a bang this time. She thought back to Jess's description of the noise but this was more like… murmurs. The last time this happened was the night before she was kidnapped. Was it going to happen again? She couldn't be sure about anything. She heard them again and she could be sure that they were speaking, but what were they saying? "Save Jess. Just save her. Please…" What? They appeared before her. These little creatures looked like flying balls of light. Souls… Lynette remembered. The night of her kidnap, she woke in the middle of the night because she thought she had heard something - a bang? Jess had heard one too. "Oh God!" she thought to herself. Was she going to lose her one and only friend? The girl who actually cared about her and treated her like she was still normal?

Jess stared out of her window. She had seen a grey man in the street, hobbling by then just staring at her. She rushed out of her house and down the street. "Tell Lynette." She thought to herself. "Run. Just run." She turned a corner and then stopped abruptly. She couldn't go down the alley, if she went down the alley there could be more trouble – she had forgotten how dangerous her area could be. She turned around only to find a chest blocking her way. She looked up to face the man with the rotten smile. "Sorry." She murmured. She took a step forward but the man grabbed her arm. Fear rushed through Jess' body like lightning. The man didn't say anything. He only looked at her with a crooked grin. It terrified her that he didn't talk. He only smiled. Then she saw them, the balls of light before her… souls?

Lynette sped down the lane, swiped her card through the door and waited. She waited for Jess but Jess never showed up. "I'm too late." She cried out to the souls. What was she doing? She had let the souls lead her to another place so that Jess would be further and further and further and further… "No you're not. Follow us." They said in unison. Lynette followed their murmurs but still, deep in her gut, she didn't trust them.

The main room was dingy and dark. Jess sat there in someone else's filth. It stank so much that she could feel herself passing out. Was her throat closing up? She looked over her body and gasped at all the cuts and bruises. This man had etched words in her skin using a knife. One said "Lynette", another, "revenge". Was this the man that did everything that harmed Lynette? A sharp knife suddenly made contact with her thigh. Jess screamed. "Tell me everything that you know about Lynette." He said with menace. "What? No!" Jess screamed. The knife went further into her skin. "You will tell me everything you know about Lynette. She broke my son's heart and he then committed suicide. How do you think I feel about her? I would've done more damage to her if those things hadn't appeared. She was lucky. I won't pretend I'm not going to enjoy this Jess." He wheezed, tapping the knife blade lightly with his finger. Jess gasped. Not through pain but through amazement. There were more and more souls appearing but they seemed to be concealing something, a person. Lynette! The souls had created a force field and … wait… what were the words that Lynette screaming. "Run, Jess just run! Get away now! I am right behind you! Run because your life depends on it."

Jess ran. Suddenly she found herself blinded by a bright light. She felt her feet lift off the ground. What was happening? She turned around and saw Lynette flying behind her and Lynette was smiling but she wasn't moving. What was happening? Jess screamed as the man shrivelled into a knot of snakes. There were two punctures in Lynette's left ankle. "No!" Jess screamed as Lynette fell to the floor in a heap. She tried to force herself out of her cage of souls but kept going backwards. Out of the dark room and into the fresh air. She fell to the floor and tears streamed down her face. Lynette was gone and there was nothing that Jess could do. She looked up and saw two pale feet in front of her. She raised her head and saw Lynette's long blonde hair. Her smiling face beamed down on Jess's face. "Remember me." Lynette said. "Never give up on life because I am gone…" The ground started to rumble and the soil opened with a deafening crack. Lynette fell through and Jess caught a glimpse of intense crimson light before the ground closed up again.

…

"Oh. She's so beautiful Charlie. She's an angel! Can we call her Lynette?" Jess asked. She had just had a long a tiresome labour but now she was holding the new Lynette in her hands. Lynette's sparkling eyes gazed up at her mothers. "Of course we can. Hello, Lynette! " said Charlie waving down at the tiny brown eyes. Lynette Kingsley. It had a nice feel about it. It was nice when you said it. Perfect.

The brown eyes, meanwhile, were watching a faint light dancing outside the window.

The Voice Inside
Jade Stanbury

I stood there like a statue; I didn't twitch while the leaves blew around the place. The trees looked like monsters and they sounded like they were whispering about me. The cat just lay on his back with his eyes open, staring into space; it looked dead and helpless. I didn't care at all. I walked off without a care in the world and I went home.

I'm Jade; I'm 13 and silent. I keep myself to myself. I have no friends. People think I'm different. Well I'm not, I'm a human like everyone else. I'm not a freak. When they call me 'freak' I get so angry. All I want to do is kill, Kill, KILL! And that's no trouble at all. I don't think I told you but I have evil voices in my head, but maybe I did tell you. I mean, I'm talking to you and you're not really so maybe you're one of them. I'm scared one day I'll listen.

I went to a family gathering at my granddad's house and my whole family was there, with jumbo hotdogs and lamb kebabs and loads of kids and conversation. I came across my auntie talking to my uncle about me they said "she's like the devil's daughter, she pure evil. Jade needs Jesus". My blood was boiling and my heart was pumping fast.

Then, like always, I tried to calm myself by reciting Hamlet in my head but this was too much. This time it wasn't working.

There was only one way to put an end to this.

To be or not to be?

Persephone
Zara McKinlay

i.

The last thing I wanted to happen to me that Saturday was to be kidnapped by some freaky, death-obsessed psycho – especially when the psycho just happened to be the Greek God of the Underworld ... Trust me, NOT COOL. My name is Persephone Harper, I am 16 years old, my mother is Demeter Harper, CEO of 'HARVEST-R' (call now to get your free information pack) and I was living in London until a few months ago, when my life changed in a matter of minutes.

"That would look great on you Seph!" exclaimed Liz. We were shopping in Kings Road at the time. I nodded and replied: "Do you mind if I pop next door? I saw some wicked heels that I want to try on.""Go ahead; I'll meet you there in 20 minutes."I walked out of the shop, blissfully unaware of the danger that was looming. I was about to cross the road when suddenly a muscular arm swooped down and swung me into the air. Before I was aware of what was happening, I was on the back of a motorbike. What kind of freak would pull someone onto their bike? If I wasn't me, I would probably have passed out from the shock and all, instead I had RAGE. I tried to shout at him, but my voice was drowned out by the roaring noise of the bike. In return, a helmet was slammed down onto my head. Thanks!

The psycho dude rapidly turned a corner, with me clinging on, and as we passed a 'DANGER, DO NOT PASS' sign, my anger instantly transformed into something maybe approaching fear – countless questions were buzzing in my head. Who was he? Where was he taking me? Why me? Why never Liz?

The guy had obviously noticed the sign too because he kept glancing behind him. Suddenly, we accelerated and it became horribly clear why this place was off limits. A huge crater, the width of the lane, blocked our path. I realised that we were heading straight for it. I braced myself for the drop - that's when I blacked out.

---

ii.

"Persephone, welcome to the Underworld!", a booming voice announced. Seriously? That psycho had dragged me all the way to the Underworld? I was just like "wah?" I scrambled to my feet and took a look at my kidnapper. He was dressed in a black motorbike jacket, studded with what looked like black diamonds, ripped black jeans. black boots. His hair was long and straggly, and black. Typical.

"Who are you? Have I been kidnapped?"

He spread out his muscular arms and smiled weirdly; "My

name is Hades, Greek God of the Underworld." My mouth must have been open because he laughed – now that was something you didn't want to hear. His voice boomed around the bare stone room. "I rescued you because I love you", he said, equally powerfully. "I have been watching you for some time now, and it became imperative that I made you mine." Eeeew!! I could have puked on the spot. I was completely grossed out. He was pretty much officially the worst guy ever and he was like three billion times my age, although his eyes were kind of nice. THAT was his pick-up tactic. How's about some social skills? But then again, I suppose the God of the Underworld doesn't get out much.

"I am sure you would like a tour of your new home!"Whoa this guy was serious! I didn't fancy living with some slimy Goth. Underworld clothes are so dreary.

He looked disgustingly creepy when he smiled: he had grey, glowing teeth! He snapped his fingers and a silvery carpet appeared in front of us. "Climb on my dear", he said, offering to help me up, but I swatted his hand away, repulsed. Hades whispered: "throne room", and suddenly, the carpet shuddered into action. We were flying so fast, and with nothing but to hold on to but the edge of the carpet, I felt very unstable and disorientated. Within seconds, we reached a vast room. It was like nothing I had ever seen before. A stone marble chamber decorated in an ancient Greek style, with ornate stone statues scattered around, and a glittering, grey mosaic floor. But the main focus was a colossal, black throne, engraved with images of spirits and demons, straining to get out. As much as it was awesome, it also felt rather bare and cold. Those winged mutt statues could have done with a wooly waistcoat, or a pillow on their head. Hades walked over to me. "I think it is time you went to sleep, you have had a busy day." To my surprise, I yawned.

---

iii.

That night I dreamt of my mother. "Persephone, where are you? Is this a game? Oh Persephone where are you?" I felt a pang of guilt. I should have never gone out. The scene in my dream changed: my mother was outside dressed in sombre black rags, instead of her usual cheery work clothes. She was on the street and her voice sounded hoarse. I could feel her desperation, her hunger to see me. My heart raced. What was happening? My mother was crumbling before me and there was nothing I could do. The dream zoomed in on a field next to my mother, the crops were wilting and yellow, the cattle and sheep wandered around, some lying dead on the ground. Once again, the scene changed and I was in a supermarket. The shelves were bare and there were signs plastered up on the windows reading 'CLOSED, NO FOOD'. I somehow sensed that this was connected to my mother – but how? Then my dream finished.

I woke up feeling incredibly anxious. I raced out of my room and into the throne room – I needed to tell Hades. When I arrived his face was full of concern. "Persephone, you have certainly kept us waiting – it has been a week." A whole week? That couldn't be possible. I dismissed that thought though, and started to tell Hades of my dream. As I did, his eyes glowed amber and his face became contorted with rage but his voice was strangely calm. "You shall not leave. You shall not speak of this again. You are needed."I started to protest but he silenced me. His eyes were stormy but I could see his face had softened.

"My Lord… one of Hypnos's servants has escaped again", a nervous spirit whispered into Hades's ear. Immediately his face hardened again. "Persephone, take a seat on your throne whilst I sort this out." He gestured to his throne. Beside it was a silver throne with flowers carved into it. It was kind of cute!

As I sat, running my fingers over the smooth carvings on the arm rests, a spirit offered me a slice of pizza and a coke. My stomach rumbled and I realised I was starving. I took the pizza and picked off the pieces of pepperoni, but the food turned to ash in my mouth. In shock, I dropped the pizza on the floor and it vanished. The glass of coke smashed and disappeared as well. I stared in disbelief at the floor. First banished from my mother and now this? What kind of hell was this? Oh yeah. The Greek

Underworld.

I decided to find Hades. Maybe I could talk some sense into him. Tip-toeing down the hall, I heard Hades's voice coming from a room labelled 'CONFERENCE B'. Not exactly what you'd expect to see in the Underworld, I thought. I pressed my ear to the door feeling a little bit guilty for eavesdropping, but knowing that I had to find out what was going on.

"This is for real Hades. Unless we can persuade Demeter to take care of the earth again – our people will die." Demeter? My mother is a Goddess? What else didn't I know? "Zeus is right Hades; do you want the Underworld to become overcrowded again? Remember the Black Death ...", a woman's voice added. Their faces scrunched."I'm not promising anything." Hades's voice sounded gruff and irritated. "Return the girl", said the woman. "Demeter's happiness will be restored. Our people will live. Death rates will be normal."Me? The Gods were on my side? I was even more eager to hear now!"Never. I love her and I want to marry her."I felt like retching again.

"Hades, you know Persephone doesn't love you and won't marry you. Be reasonable. Wisdom is the key." The woman's voice was calm and hypnotic. Her charm was clearly working on Hades too, because he finally listened. "Fine. I will return her if she hasn't eaten any food whilst she's been here. You know the rule. If she has eaten anything in the Underworld, she must stay here forever.""Go and fetch her then. We'll ask her."In horror, I ran as fast as I could away from the room. I had been so close to returning to my mother and I had blown it. Aghast with myself, I sat wondering what would happen to me. Curses to my childhood of free room service!

Suddenly the demon who had offered me the pizza sprang up next to me. "Lord Hades will see you now."Swallowing, I nodded and walked towards my fate. The door groaned as I pushed it open, the noise pretty much summing up how I felt. The demon wafted in the doorway, making me even more uneasy. Not to be judgemental but demons are jerks!

Hades was sat on a black recliner chair, in front of a giant screen. Twelve people were staring straight at me and I realised that these were the Gods. "Um, hi!", I said, not knowing what else to say. Twenty-three eyes blinked."Persephone, we have a very important question to ask you which will determine your fate. Have you eaten any food since your arrival at the Underworld?"I gulped and replied, "I haven't touched a single crumb." Hades's face fell and the other Gods' faces lit up."Oh yes you did, you ate a slice of pizza, I saw you", croaked the demon in the doorway."No, no! I was so thirsty I just swallowed a few pieces of pepperoni!" I protested, desperate to be freed."That's enough!" bellowed Hades."Please, Hades," begged Hera. "Let her go for a while! A few slices of pepperoni are barely a side-dish."Twentry-three eyebrows raised at Hades. Hades shrugged, defeated.

"All right. Persephone may go back to her mother. But for half of every year, she must return to the Underworld!"

The flying carpet appeared by my side. "Go my dear, before he changes his mind," said Hera. I hopped on and the carpet jerked into life, revving like a motorbike. And so I returned to my mother.

iv.

I gave up all my cool and sobbed like a baby in my mum's eyes. I told her about the kidnapping and the Underworld and the bargain I was forced to accept with Hades.

"I thought as much," she said, but told me not to worry. Her words soothed me. With mum here I knew that things would be alright. Next, I had to phone Liz, who must have been worried sick. She recovered a little too quickly and started telling me about some cute new boy at school.

A week passed and news spread about the miraculous end to the world-wide famine. Mum was back at work. The world was rejoicing and I knew that somewhere the gods were too. But on the downside, it meant sprouts and broccoli again for dinner, yuck! I hate greens! I guess the grass is always greener on the other side!

A Fading Light
i. Matilda Murray

I woke up to find that some of my chickens had disappeared in the middle of the night. At first I thought that it was some thieves, but I soon realised that there were feathers scattered everywhere and a pile of bones lay at the edge of the fence. This could only have been an animal.

I looked closely at the sand, and saw faint paw prints. Their familiar shape suggested a wolf, but they were too large to belong to an average sized wolf, or even an alpha male. So what could it have been? I looked; disposed of the carcasses the beast had left behind, and went in to town to buy a trap to catch this thing, whatever it was.

For days and nights, I waited in anticipation for the animal, but every morning when I woke, I would find the trap empty and the chickens unharmed. Once or twice the postman came but I had no time to sort through bills and my back tensed at the clink of my letterbox.

On the night of a full moon something strange happened. In the morning I woke up to find myself sleeping in the cage that I had set up for the wolf. What could have happened? I looked around and saw the same footprints I had seen last month. I counted my chickens and realised that two were missing. Could the beast have dragged me from my bed and into the chicken shed? My skirt was torn. Perhaps it had a sense of humour. Perhaps I was lucky to be alive.

Months after months, I would wake up, after the night of a full moon, to find myself stuck in the cage. It would take me a full hour to pick the lock. I decided to set up a video camera to catch the beast in action. I would record everything that was going to happen on the coming night.

The next morning, I watched myself approaching the video camera and knocking it to the floor, and I was shocked to see what I had found. The video buzzed and cracked then settled on the blank wall of my bedroom. I watched as my shadow bent at the stomach, in seeming agony, and grew to monstrous proportions. As I had begun to suspect, I was the beast.

It took me some hours to recover from my discovery. Did this run in my blood? The gene most probably lay dormant unless triggered by something. By killing somebody? Was this my punishment?

Every full moon I would lock myself up, but it was no use, I always managed to get free. The villagers started to suspect something when their livestock started to go missing. They came as one, lead by the postman. I was drinking tea when the shouts began. I watched a little girl throw stones at my window. I put my cup down on the saucer. I knew I had to leave and find my own peace in the forest.

ii. Robbie Masters

Ribbons of moonlight flowed down its furry coat, like a carpet in the mist. The wolf lurked through the lonely forest, creeping towards the castle's great doors, along the leafy path.

I could hardly see anything, just a black silhouette. I squinted as I saw the silhouette shape into a human. The figure opened the stunning, great doors and slammed them shut as it disappeared within. I followed it into the house; the first thing I saw was a book shelf, I ran a finger along some of the titles and illustrations: "Call of the Wild", "Little Red Riding Hood". I heard the sound of metallic steps, as I turned frantically I managed to catch a foot slip out of sight on the spiral staircase of the main tower. I tried to run after it, but by the time I got upstairs there was no sign of anything. I leaned up onto the window to catch my breath and watched the moon shine its web across the whole forest. A gust of wind had come up behind me, or else every lantern on the stairs had run out of fuel. I watched them die in order, top to bottom, taking me into deeper and deeper darkness.

---

iii. Mary Beaty

SEEK

This was the killer night, the night she lost everything. Jack stood, they stood, unsuspecting victims of a terrible force. In the shadows a furred creature lay, planning the route, the place, the pounce, the kill. Still Jack stood watching the stars with her warm hand in his. Slowly, one step at a time, the breathing calm, a devilish monster leapt and Jack lay torn on the floor. The immortal next went for the girl. Its claws scraped down her left arm. Yet somehow she escaped. She sat and wept as every cell of her body grew cold with pain. Dark stains of blood grew across her cocktail dress. She could not contemplate the seriousness of her situation.

STALK

Thoughts drifted around her head as she trudged back to the room she called home. Once again that dreadful night swirled in her mind. The dark claw, the screaming pain. Jack was gone forever. Many years of happiness. Many years together. All gone in the blink of an eye. Now he lay under her feet and above her head. Mourning, the tears dripped off her pale cheeks. She was like ice, melting under a black sky, suffocating her. Love, loneliness, loss. If only he were here. It seemed too soon, too sudden. But that is what death is like, displeasing.

Night crept in as she sat on her bed, staring into the distance. Hours had passed and nothing had changed. She slumped to the floor and lay there still, as if lifeless. But inside a change was growing. Soon the transformation would be complete. Soon a new beast would rise out of the anger and hurt, once more hunting to kill.

The yellow eyes, the acute teeth, the quick mind, the once weak and lost heart of this tormented beast, driven to insanity, to the brink of death, was now returning, blood thirsty.

The sun crept through the open curtain. Her life was changing dramatically. By now she was on her hands and knees, frantically scratching at the rough wooden floor boards. She was trying to hold back her own strength, her own power of mind. She leapt across the room in a frantic rage, smashing into the wall on the other side. Howling she lifted her head to the roof, screaming in her own language. A wolf from within, straining against the human heart's resistance.

A knock on the door disrupted her distant thoughts. She snapped back to her old self and to her familiar thoughts. Outside he called, warned, threatened then burst through the door. A jail awaited her arrival. An empty cell, all for her.

Insane he said, mad. Lost her mind. His words hit her

like wooden paddles, enraging her. Maybe it was true, but they did not understand that her peace was forever disrupted and lost.

SEIZE

The cell was cold and empty. Only a wooden bed and metal bars. The door was shut and locked. She was trapped, not only in an empty dungeon but in her own sorrow too. She needed him. Without him she was lost, a lone wolf running free but feeling caught. She felt like she should give herself up to the pack; let them control her in their own bizarre ways.

SUFFOCATE

"Guilty in the name of the law. The neighbourhood's peace disrupted by her unlawful behaviour. Her peace forever ruined. Why would they not understand? She needed him. His ground was restful where she was not. She did not understand this cage or its strange shadows.

She could hear every word, see everything, but could not understand why she was here. She was fading in the light of the moon. Scratching, clawing, and howling, she needed air, needed the night. Her claws could break the metal bars that caught her but somehow she would still be trapped.

CONSUME

As she leapt out of the small window, the sirens raised

awareness of the escapee. The short fur of her back ruffled in the wind. Rapidly racing across the fields towards the safety of the woods. Finally the cover of the woods lay all round her. She gazed in amazement at the leafy trees that towered above her. Her humble home looked golden in the falling darkness. The autumn colours wet with rain. She couldn't wait, or they'd be upon her, so she ran on. Through the darkness, a shadowy figure tearing through the bracken and leaves.

The stone barely reached above the muddy ground, its colour and dignity slowly fading. It was a mark of love and hope but now it marked his place. She dug down to where he lay still and quiet. Her now human hands reaching down to pull the limp, lifeless body out. His body like a ragdoll, not used for hundreds of years. She dragged him to the river where she lay him down on the sand bank, panting.

His heart was inviting. It would only take one bite to be unclasped. Her teeth were sharp enough and she knew she could do it if she could only persuade herself to. Now was the time to do it. One bite. Her teeth sank into his chest and pulled out his heart. His once white shirt now drowned in black blood. His body wilting in sorrow.

After, he would float down the river till some unsuspecting soul finds the body without its heart and perhaps buries it in a new place. She however would roam free forever.

Her last human words were spoken. A wolf who has been lost for many years, now found place in a girl. His heart; her first wolf meal and her invitation to the pack. Her first human kill will change the world. She is the pack leader of a fading pack, a fading light.

They Took Her Away
Tainton Cole

Long toenails poked out of my dirty sandals as I walked through the dusty, dark park on a cold and misty winter day. The only good thing about this walk was that I had my striking wife, Julia, at my side. Her dark, greasy hair swishing in the wind. Although it was dark, with her at my side the sky lit up like the sun was rising on the horizon. She made me feel like I was in a trance, as if I was falling down a rainbow. She pulled me closer and whispered in my ear: "It's time to go..."

We reached our home, a basement flat in the rough end of town. Mouldy dark green windows greeted us. I twisted the handle of the cold, damp door and walked in, then immediately flopped on the sofa. My wife did not. I did not take any notice of this. Julia had recently been diagnosed with schizophrenia. She's not mad, just different - that's why I married her. A few minutes later she came and sat down with me. I told her, "I love you". She didn't speak, I held her closer and she didn't move. All Julia did was stand up and drag herself to the bedroom.

I woke up the next day to the sound of the door slamming. I looked to my left to find that she wasn't there, my heart started to pound. I rushed downstairs and ran outside barefoot, looking around frantically. It was just a normal day, car horns beeping, the bin men dragging plastic bins around, pigeons pecking the pavement. I stepped down the stairs and there she was, my Julia, standing across the road. I waited at the traffic lights to go and get her, but a big lorry went past and she was gone…like magic. Suddenly everything started to spin and I saw a silhouette of a person standing in front of me. "Julia?", I asked, trying to blink out the spinning and rushing in my head. I looked down and noticed a syringe sticking out of my thigh.

"What the…"

Two massive potato hands clasped me by the shoulders and the world span more ferociously. My legs wobbled and I didn't know if I was standing up anymore. Through crossed, squinting eyes, I saw two hazy figures above me, and heard the voice from one of them, "Come on, Hank. You're coming with us".

"I haven't done anything wrong", I mumbled, now unsure if I even had any legs. "Where's Julia?"

...

I woke up in a cell. A big black door in front of me and a tiny glass window on my left. My vision was clearer and all my limbs were intact, thankfully. I couldn't believe the mistake that they had made, they must have confused me with someone else. My stomach churned with worry for Julia. There was a knock at the door, and a short man entered, with a brown jacket and a concerned face.

"Hi there, Hank", he said, with the same concerned face.

"Excuse me, but can I ask what the hell is going on? I haven't done anything wrong and actually I really need to go and find my wife - she's not well and shouldn't be left alone. Please could you let me go now?"

The man's face had crumpled more in concern, so much so that his eyebrows were meeting in the middle. At that precise moment Julia appeared at the tiny window. I rushed over to her. "Julia! Hello, can you hear me? What's going on?!" But she just stared through the window with a blank expression, her eyes silently weeping.

"What have you done to her?" I demanded. "Have you drugged her? You are thugs. You're the thugs who've been circling our house for the last month aren't you?"

"Hank..."

"Can you let me out?! That's my wife, there! I need to see her. Is she ok? Why am I here?" A growing sense of panic was spreading across my body, hot waves of fear whooshing up my neck and down to my feet. This all too familiar feeling was coming back to me now, my stomach twisting into knots and my mouth turning to cotton wool, my heart pounding to the beat of the overwhelming dread filling my brain and body. I knew where I was.

"Hank... You don't have a wife".

"This is my wife, don't you see her? Julia, Julia! It's Hank, I'm here. We have to get home."

"Hank... You live here. This is your home, we look after you."

My mouth began to scream, my fists pounded the window. I knew where I was.

The Moon
Kiya Weekes

L eft to die alone. The breeze as still as untouched water, slowly rippling past, she stood and stared, her pale face resembled the moon, alone in the night. Long black hair flew back, pulling into the wind, as if taken aback by her beauty. Full of quiet emotion, she stood there waiting, waiting for something. She didn't know what, but she stayed, savouring the pain forming in her toes.

The wind grew colder, the sky grew darker, she grew older and maybe duller, but no wiser. Her black eye makeup was knocked streaming down her face by dew drops from the thin leaves above, leaving a trail of its being. Her ripped gloves didn't do much for her warmth. She heard something in the distance. She could not know what it was but maybe this was the something she was waiting for.

To her dismay nothing came; nothing but a piece of paper, too faded, too caught up in the wind and only half remembered; somehow too trivial to read. She lay on the grass, the only brightness in this scene, the moon.

Her face grew paler, she grew tired. She stared once more at the moon, she walked closer to it. There was the end. She could reach out and press against it. She couldn't love, she was alone. She took one further step, she lost her footing and let herself fall, tumbling, tumbling over the edge. What were her last words? She wrote them down perhaps? Maybe *no matter how far I'm pushed I will always be by your side,* or maybe something else.

She lay still, untouchable, her black hair spread over her face, over the ground.

Over.

The black eye make-up, like vines over her pale delicate face, the true image of great sadness. Alone, she was left. Left to die alone.

Little Girl Lost
i. Amie Carter

I should have known this was coming. From the first sign. I should have known. Here I am in this sweltering dark room, here's what I know now.

One day at a family BBQ I was in the garden sunbathing with my cousins running all around. I started to smell a weird smell of gas and coal. I looked to my left, waiting for my eyes to adjust from the sun. I saw a girl dressed in rags. She started to sing a nursery rhyme, *ring a ring a roses,* rocking on our neighbour's swing chair. She shocked me for some reason. I didn't think our neighbour had a child. She dressed in a long ragged dress in dark faded grey and purple, she was covered in soot dust and dirt. Then she gradually turned her head and stared at me, all was silent... and then when I blinked she'd gone. When she had disappeared I kept thinking of her face. I couldn't get the image out of my head, her eyes were brown, the same colour as her hair, but they were filled with resentment. Her hair was long and taken over with knots. Her face was thick with scars that made her seem always angry but innocent at the same time. I noticed the storm clouds after she left, thick and knotted like her hair. Next I went in , forgetting the sunshine. I didn't tell anyone about what just happened but I'm regretting it now.

As I walked inside, hearing my dad complain about the weather man saying it would be sunny all day, my mum said to me " what's the matter dear?"

"Nothing " I replied. I looked outside. But all I could see was the thick fain and the clouds exploding.

I tried to forget about what happened and just move on with my life, and I did. It wasn't until about two months later around 22:00. I was looking into the mist of the night sky gazing at the moon as a form dived into my eyes, she appeared again…

She was standing in my garden sitting in a chair staring at the moon too, sing the same song, *a pocket full of posies*, then she disappeared again, fading into the mist.

Next morning I told my mum and dad about last night my mum said " I just had a bad dream that's all." Man were they wrong.

I told myself it was a dream and I managed to convince myself it was.

Later that day I was on my way back from the shops. I was eating a lollipop. Then I heard her singing I couldn't see her just hear her, " *ring a ring a roses"*, I looked around trying to find her but the singing stopped. Where had I seen her before?

---

ii. Freya Miller

As the wind nipped my fingertips, my face was being gnawed at
by the hungry cold as bones are gnawed by dogs. Foxes ran this
way and that as Jack Frost crept in coating every inch of the city
with a shimmering silver glow. Endeavouring to make it home
without getting frostbite, I hastened my stride.

Many people have talked about Miscellaneous Lane, there
have been stories about how ghosts supposedly appeared. I
thought it was just a figment of people's imaginations, or a story
made up to explain disappearances which probably happened on
the other side of the city.

In my quest to get home I decided to take the lane as a short
cut to my usual route. I could see to the end of the lane with the
dim street light illuminating the street beyond. I took one
nervous step into the dark depths that would lead me to my
queries. As I delved deeper I could see dilapidated houses with
boarded windows and holes in the walls, big enough for only
mice to get through. Ivy clung to the brickwork like veins on an
old man's hand and as I walked past it seemed to be dying,
shrivelling up and dying. How was it possible?

The wind started to pick up. I looked up into the fog,
beyond, a dark figure was standing, surrounded by a veil of mist.
I convinced myself that it was my imagination, but as I crept
forward I started to have doubts, for there stood little Martha. I

remembered the news reports. She went missing three days ago. You would have had to be deaf not to have heard about it, but then you still would have read it in every newspaper. Tentatively I stepped closer, even though I knew who this was, I wasn't sure if all was well. She opened her eyes and my suspicions were confirmed, staring back at me were two blood red orbs.

My eyes were locked on her threatening gaze unable to look away; my vision was taken over by her. I could see Martha running, running, running. She was looking around frantically, and then the image of a children's playground appeared, deserted from all life, a noise could be heard. Laughing, children laughing. Her eyes returned to the blood red colour that reflected my trembling body as the playground scene faded away like mist, revealing the decrepit lane. Tears rolled down her face. Just as I felt unsure what to do, she murmured

"What is happening to me?"

I was unable to reply. My sympathy subsided when the fury gripped her feeble body.

My feet wouldn't move, my whole body was fixed to my spot on Miscellaneous Lane.

I wish I could have helped poor Martha, but as my family weeps and my only love marries another, woman all that is left is a rose sprouted from the ivy that hangs over my resting place and drips blood from Its shining petals.

iii. Ethan Connoly

I have to find my family
we were on holiday
when the plane crashed
landing in Nokuma
and I lost them.
I passed out
and have no idea what time it is,
but I have to find shelter
quickly or I will freeze.
I will trudge through the thick snow
until I get to a small village
and ask if they have
some old shack where I could sleep
and I will ask if they have
seen them–
my sister and my dad.

---

iv. Georgia Young.

Where was I? Everywhere I looked there was snow; snow over here next to more snow over there. A few weeks ago I would have dreamed for a place like this, no noise, no disturbances. No! Not now. No phone. No clue. I just wanted to be at home with my mum my brother, working in front of the fire, drinking hot cocoa, my usual routine. Something then caught my eye. An old village. I ran , soaking my boots in melting snow. A village full of shops. They all looked open but there were no customers inside and, come to think of it, no shopkeepers. I kept walking. I heard a scream. "Hello is anyone there?" I muttered. I got no reply. My heart was pumping like never before. I thought it was going to spill out of my mouth. At the end of the village I saw an old ruined square. There stood a figure. I didn't feel so alone anymore. I screamed to see if she'd notice me. "Is anyone there?" she shouted with the cold smoke coming out of her old wrinkled mouth. "Yes, yes me!" I replied. "Oh…hello dear" she smiled happily. "Can you help me please?" I asked. "Yes dear, of course I can" she said helpfully. "I need to get back to London, do you know how I can?" My hands started to shake; tears started to form in my eyes. As they trickled down my face, my mascara went with them. My chin shivered making a clacking sound as my teeth clenched together. "Sorry darling I don't know how you get to London, I only know how to get into

The Town and home" she said apologetically. "Okay well…thank you for your time" I smiled. "No problem" the withered fragile lady replied. Feeling hopeless I walked away.

I walked and walked with all of these thoughts flying round in my head! Is my mum okay? Am I ever going to get home? Would there be news from hospital? Had mum been discharged? Was she gathering wood for our fire? Was she gathering a search party? My face would be all over the news.

As I dragged my feet along the floor in this dark strange village, I saw a forest. Why had I not seen it from the snow hills? As I approached I imagined the branches were arms ready to grab anyone that wondered in. You could hear the hum from all of the lost villagers. "Ring-a-ring-a-roses a pocket full of posies". I had never been this scared before in my life, it was like watching a film, a horror movie. Trying to stay calm, I began to hum. I saw dozens of white forms flying around me. What kind of a place was this? Maybe if I hummed along to their song, these spirits would not hurt me. I imagined I saw my nan. I squinted my eyes to try and see from if it was really her. I saw her slowly flying towards me, gradually getting closer and closer. When she finally approached me she grabbed my soft brown hair and lifted me up. My emotions were mixed: scared, angry, relieved. When she let go I tried to run, but the old lady from the town was there. She grabbed my legs and dragged me along the floor. Her face was as peaceful as the snow. My mum told me; if something bad happened, scream and hopefully someone would hear. I screamed and screamed. No one was coming to help me. I lay on the floor trying to catch my breath. She flew over me, skimming my face. I brought my knees up to my chest. I glanced round to see if I could find her. Nowhere to be seen. Silently I stood up. She came behind me grabbing me by my ears and whispered "Do you wish to say goodbye before you leave your friends and family?". "That's enough!" I shouted. I wriggled and I wriggled. She let go. I dropped 20ft from the air. "I love you mum" I squealed. As I hit the floor I saw nothing but darkness and I felt no pain. But I felt something.

---

v. Charli Eglinton

Over the moor she wanders, a faint distant shadow,

Listen hard enough, you hear her cry,

Please don't try and help,

Don't follow her voice, don't follow her footsteps,

Don't look her in the eye,

Cover your ears when she speaks, kick off the cover of her pain

Ignore her cries for help, ignore them,

Her sobbing is in vain,

But you've listened and you've followed,

Saw her as she saw you

I had done the same

Over the moor she wanders,

Listen hard enough, you hear her cry,

If only you listened to what I said.

I tried to warn you but now there's no time

And you're wandering again

After the little girl in red.

--The End--

Thank You!

This was always a risky venture. When the RPAYP team did the market research for this project, we could not find anyone else doing what we were doing. Was this because we had created something daring and original or was this all just an inherently bad idea? The haunt of this uncertainty was our biggest obstacle from the start. Time after time we almost ended it all because we doubted we could raise the money, produce something of quality or gain the interest of our readers. Without the sudden and often unexpected help of all those who came out to support us, you would not be reading this book.

First, we would like to thank the 45 backers who funded this project, and its future manifestations on kickstarter.com. In particular **Lea Heron** who has not only been generous here but has consistently supported the school and its initiatives in different ways for many years. Equally, we would like to thank **Mona Adams** and **Anne Hahlo,** who not only donated generously, but also gave up time to publicize the project.

Second, we would like to thank **Sarah Cox** who gave valuable advice and edited our campaign video.

Third, a gigantic thanks to **Cara Quinn Larkin** whose commitment to her year group is simply immense. She has supported this project every step of the way, from helping to direct our video to enlisting the backing for a quarter of our required funds. We were touched and inspired by the efforts of **Sheldon Gabriel** and **Margaret Quinn** in spreading the word about this project. Thank you to **Joan, Sheila and Joy Lynch,** Mrs Quinn's neighbours in Ireland who showed us we have supporters all around the world!

Last of all, thank you to all others we have not mentioned here who helped, in whatever small way, along the way. And thank you to you, our reader, for your time and trust in reading this book.

Thank You! RPA Young Publishers, 2013.
